MURDER
IN
COSTA RICA

L.D. MARKHAM

MURDER IN COSTA RICA
By L.D. Markham
Copyright © 2018 Lynda D Markham
Cover Art by Karen Phillips
All rights reserved.

This is a work of fiction. Names, characters, places, brands, media, and incidents are either the product of the author's imagination or are used fictitiously, and any resemblance to actual persons, living or dead, businesses, companies, events, or locales is entirely coincidental.

Thank you for purchasing this book and supporting an indie author.
Visit us at ldmarkhambooks.com

Inspired by true events
Viva Jairo Mora Sandoval

DEDICATION

To Mom and Dad thanks for always believing in me.

To Fred thanks for your love, support, encouragement, and being my sounding board through this adventure.

Chapter 1

Costa Rica:

Alma checked a turtle location on the dark beach when three men came into view, moonlight gleaming off assault rifles. She turned but her bare feet had no traction on the sand. Her heart raced, every inch of her screaming danger. Heavy breaths trailed too close behind. A fist struck her temple, white spots dotting the sky as she landed face-first in the sand, the barrel of a gun shoved into her back.

"Don't move."

Raising her hands she gave up her struggle. The man grabbed her by the hair with one hand and stuffed an oily tasting cloth into her mouth with the other. Before she could register what was happening, her hands were tied behind her back and her face pushed into the sand again. On her knees with her bottom more up than down, her shorts were pulled from her and she felt the weight of a heavy man force himself onto her.

With her neck held to the ground, Alma couldn't fight, she couldn't move. Sand burned into her knees as she gasped for air. The smell of the cloth made her ill. The only noise was a squeak coming from her gag as she tried to scream. *Why did I come alone?* she thought. Pushing her over when he was through with her, he threatened, "If I see you on this beach again, you're dead. Tell everyone to go home. No one will be safe here."

In a fetal position, she saw he had a ski mask over his face, dark eyes, and clothes to match. She lay stunned and in pain for several minutes, her body shivering in fright. She managed to wiggle her way out of the bindings and back into her shorts. She was just beyond the Playa Soledad turtle hatchery.

When she was able to get up, she moved toward the hatchery for help. Once there, she saw the other volunteers had been tied and gagged as well. Coolers and boxes that held turtle eggs from their explorations that night were on their side and empty. No one at the hatchery had been able to move. She removed their gags and untied them, but no one had phones to make an emergency call. The men had taken them. She wasn't sure how many men had done this, but they were now long gone. They walked as a group to the street trying to flag down a motorist who would help.

She would call Gabriel, make a report and promised herself she would never come back to Playa Soledad again. She would pray for peace and security to return to the beach.

San Francisco:

Laura heard a choking noise somewhere near her. Slowing her pace from a jog to a walk, she looked around and discovered a baby sea lion hiding in some brush off to the side of her running trail. "Hey little guy, what are you doing way over here? Are you lost?" She scanned the area to see if the mother might be nearby. There was a parking lot beyond the trail, brush, and then a busy street. No one was around who would hear her yell, and she didn't want the little guy to go beyond the brush, fearing he would get hurt.

There had been several news reports of sea lions being spotted in residential areas of San Francisco. They were having a hard time finding food and this seemed to be the reason for the sightings. Keeping her distance, she grabbed her phone and dialed the local marine mammal rescue center. *It's a good thing I decided to take a jog along the shore following that long meeting today.* Laura hated to see an animal in need and felt compelled to help by keeping an eye on the little one until the rescue crew arrived.

Once the pup was picked up and on his way to the rescue center, Laura walked to her car for the drive back to her condo. She felt satisfied helping the pup which strengthened her enthusiasm for her upcoming sustainable tourism trip.

Chapter 2

Costa Rica:

On the plane, Laura imagined walking along a sandy beach, cool water from the Caribbean lapping onshore and the sun's blanket of warmth enveloping her. *Bing bing* went off overhead. She jumped in her seat, now awake, eyes wide open. The anticipation of landing in a tropical country and being alone for several weeks wasn't the only thing keeping her from sleeping on the long flight from California.

The captain made an announcement. "…If you look to your right…" Through the window, she spotted Lake Nicaragua below and escaped back into self-reflection and memories.

"What do you think you're doing? Why can't you just go for two or three weeks like a normal traveler?" her mother had asked as she put the final preparations on dinner.

"Mom, I need to get away. I'm tired of doing what everyone else wants me to do. I need time to think. I want to explore new interests."

"You don't even speak the language!"

"I know enough Spanish to get by. Many residents speak English anyway. I'll improve my Spanish through immersion. I need a change. I need to find *me* again."

"It just seems like such a long time."

"You know I've been stressed out from work and the divorce. I can't find the joy in anything anymore, everything's a chore. I just want to have some fun and enjoy life again."

"What's so important about these sea turtles anyway, why can't you just find your fun here?" her mother sighed.

"We've been over this. It's a chance to study a new interest and enjoy a beautiful country. Remember that baby sea lion I helped? I want to do more of that. I'm over the grind of corporate America. Besides, it's not forever. It's just a couple of months, you won't even miss me."

The in-flight announcement brought her back to reality. Three months after the conversation with her mom, the plane was about to land at San José's Aero Puerto Inter-Nacional Juan Santamaría.

Laura made her way through the sterile corridor of sunlit glass walls and white marble tiles. She searched out the signs for "Leatherback Sea Turtle Conservancy."

She spotted the representative and smiled. "Hi. Laura Humphreys. Are you Daniela Segura?"

"Welcome to Costa Rica. I hope you're as excited to be here as we are to have you join our group." They shook hands and Laura thought they were about the same age. Daniela's golden brown skin appeared luminous and Laura wondered if genetics or humidity were at play.

"Thank you. I'm very excited to be here. I've been dreaming of this opportunity."

They headed for the auto park, and as the doors slid sideways the intense heat hit her like a furnace blast. In the distance, darkening grey clouds were accumulating.

Laura threw her backpack onto the backseat of Daniela's Hyundai Santa Fe and climbed in the passenger seat. "We'll be heading southeast to Puerto Limón to the home of your host family, the Valverdes. It's about a three-hour drive. You'll meet our biologist Gabriel Montenegro and some other volunteers tomorrow morning."

The Braulio Carrillo highway carved a narrow strip through the rainforest with cliffs dropping on one side. Lush tropical vegetation raced by as Laura took in the new sights "That sounds perfect. I've never seen so many different shades of green in one area. When I was in Tamarindo a couple of years ago at the end of the dry season, everything was brown and, well, dead looking."

"It's very wet on this side of the country. It gets more rain on an annual basis, plus the rainy season starts soon," Daniela looked up at the darkening sky, "It looks like we're getting an early start this year."

They arrived at the Valverdes home and Daniela introduced Laura to Clemente and Maria. Clemente was a tall brawny guy who reminded her of a giant teddy bear. He reached out his hand, "Welcome to our home." She felt protected in his presence right away.

Laura moved toward the hand-carved Guanacaste-wood barstools and viewed banana trees through the large picture window at the back of the house. "Your home is very beautiful. Thank you for letting me stay here," she said. "How far are we from the beach?"

"We're a couple of miles from Playa Soledad where you will be spending most of your time. I'll drive you there in the morning so you can get your bearings," Maria said.

Laura thought to herself *solitude beach, sounds perfect.* Daniela said her goodbyes and encouraged Laura to get to know the Valverdes, settle in and get a good night sleep. Her new adventure in sea turtle conservation would begin in the morning.

Chapter 3

Descending the church steps, Esteban thanked the priest for the morning mass. A successful businessman, respected in his community, he was tall man of Spanish descent with a paunch, deep set dark eyes, and shoulder length greasy black hair. He pushed the hair from his face as his cell phone rang. "Hola."

"Esteban, have you hired the four men I requested for the next shipment?" His business partner Wendigo's voice echoed.

"Si. I've also secured the same member of the *policía* we used last year, easy since we pay double what he makes on duty. He'll be reliable eyes on that beach," Esteban said.

"*Excelente*, I've found a property we can use in Pocora. Can you meet me there on Saturday, say around noon?"

"I'll be there. What's the address?"

***

At the Pocora location, Esteban parked and got out of his car, careful not to step in the recent rain puddles.

"One of my contacts from Mexico told me about this place. I think it serves our purposes well," Wendigo said as he showed Esteban around. "It has several acres of grass land with a few banana trees for cover. It's located away from the main road, so the buildings are hidden."

"I agree. We can use this building as the main house for the supplies." Esteban smelled peppery damp earth and walked around rusted barrels with chemical labels ripped and faded, now tipped over and empty. "We can put processing equipment here," he pointed to the front cement deck "We can use this adjacent area to store the weapons, and can keep the powder and supply bags dry over there." He waved to where a kitchen could have been located.

"Let me show you this second building. There are some bunks for the men."

Both houses were typical Costa Rican masonry with concrete flooring. Basic dry wall had been hung but the homes were half finished and looked like they'd been repurposed after being abandoned.

"Someone took time to build these bunks. The wood looks sturdy. I see no electricity or running water here. We'll have to purchase some cook stoves and I'll order some barrels and basins that we can put out for catching rain." Esteban looked at the sky and knew another round was on its way. "This will suit our needs well." Not glamorous, but more functional for the crew than many of the shacks they grew up in.

They walked another hundred yards north of the buildings, "The men will need to cut down some of the overgrowth in this area, but you will notice that there are two helipads here. Our contact can fly in to pick up deliveries once the product has been cut and processed. Make sure your men follow the instructions cutting the powder to 60 to 80 percent purity depending on the final distribution point." Wendigo said.

"I like this plan, the ideas we had back at the Universidad de Panama 15 years ago are coming to fruition. I think my men will do fine here. We should also start looking for a team on the Pacific coast."

***

Beni rolled down the passenger window in his van and called to the two guys standing outside of Mercado Central. "Hey, are you Luis and Juan Carlos?"

"Who wants to know?" Luis touched his machete sheath.

"I'm Beni. Esteban told me to pick two guys up here, you match his descriptions."

"If you're with Esteban then we're with you," Juan Carlos headed for the van's door. "I'm Juan Carlos, this is my friend Luis. Don't mind him. He's usually defensive."

"Get in, and I'll get you both to Pocora ranch. Esteban told me to show you around."

"Will he be there?"

"No. Not today. You'll only see him when he needs to provide instructions on incoming shipments. I'll be the one supervising daily. How did he find you anyway?"

"We were looking for work when he said he needed help with a job but that we'd have to live at his ranch. He bought us dinner the other night and told us to be at this spot today, said someone would come get us. He promised he had work a couple of nights a week and that we had to do some cooking also."

"We're happy to cook, but we've never had to cook anything ourselves ever," Luis said as he climbed onto the bench in the back.

Beni laughed, "The cooking you'll be doing is pretty easy. Its just a couple of ingredients. But you'll need to be careful not to sample it. That'll get you into trouble in so many ways."

Luis and Juan Carlos looked at each other. They were thrilled to have work and food and were positive they'd stay out of trouble.

Chapter 4

The sun blazed through the window. A ray seared like a laser pen into Laura's right eye. Welcome to her first full day in Costa Rica. Hadn't she just rolled over, pillow to her ears to drown out the low guttural roar of the howler monkeys? The last time she'd awakened to that noise was near Arenal Volcano on her previous trip. She sat up, remembered where she was and realized the alarm on her phone wouldn't be needed here, nature would dictate her wake up calls.

After breakfast, Maria drove her to Playa Soledad. At the beach, Laura felt the ocean breeze take a strand of her blond hair away from her face. She smiled, took a deep breath to welcome the salty air, and smelled a hint of gasoline too. Was that the port or had a boat recently been by? She also picked up the scent of damp sand mixed with a woody overtone. *They should bottle that scent,* she thought. She surveyed the area. Ground cover and a thick line of trees were framed by the ocean on the opposite side. Waves crashed over the volcanic rock that jetted out from the water to the right of her, and fluffy white cotton ball clouds were randomly placed in the blue sky. *Perfect.*

She saw a tall woman with auburn hair, and moved forward to ask if she might also be a volunteer. "Good Morning, my name is Laura Humphreys. Are you also with the Leatherback Sea Turtle Conservancy Program, LSTC?"

"Yes, I'm Bianca Alvarez," She turned to offer her hand and Laura was struck by the emerald green eyes that stood out from her pale skin and wondered if she might be a model.

"Hi Bianca, nice to meet you. Have you been here long?"

"Just a couple of weeks. I joined the program from Spain."

"How long will you be with the program?" asked Laura

"I hope to spend three months here, until my visa expires. My husband travels a lot, so I have the freedom to get away and do what I want"

"Oh, that's great. What does your husband do?"

"Julian's an investor, mostly in antiquities. Sometimes I travel with him. Sometimes I do my own thing. What about you, are you married?" Bianca turned to look carefully at Laura.

"Not anymore, that's part of the reason I'm here. Needed an escape."

"How long do you plan to be here?"

"A couple of months," Laura drew in a breath. Maybe longer, she thought.

"You are from the Estado Unidos, no?"

"Yes, I'm from Northern California. Walnut Creek. Are you familiar with that area?"

"No."

"Oh. Anyway, I look forward to focusing on the turtles and making new friends."

"Come with me and I'll introduce you to Gabriel. I should warn you, he is very passionate about his turtles and loves to talk. I'm sure he'll be eager to get you started."

***

At the hatchery, Bianca took the lead. "Gabriel, this is Laura Humphreys, our new volunteer from California."

"Welcome. We've been expecting you," Gabriel made notes on his clipboard. "I'll be the one to schedule and assign tasks to everyone. Let me give you a little tour and some basic information on what we do here." He spoke English very well with just a hint of a Spanish inflection.

"That would be great. I'd like to know a little bit about you?"

"Sure. I received my Degree in Biology from University of California-Santa Barbara, came back to Costa Rica because I grew up here." Laura tried not to stare but he had really dark skin, very bushy eyebrows, intense dark green eyes and a thin line of facial hair from lip to chin. He looked more like a kid barely out of high school. She wondered if he was part of the Afro-Caribbean culture that the Valverdes had spoken of in her brief history lesson.

Gabriel continued as they moved forward, "We are now in what we call the hatchery. You'll notice that we have the area divided into columns and rows. This is where we protect turtle eggs. All the areas will eventually be labeled with where and when the turtle eggs were collected."

"How many types of turtles will we work with? I've read that there are six species that nest in Costa Rica."

"On this beach, this time of year, we work with just the leatherback turtles officially called *Dermuchelys Coriacea*. Once the turtle has finished laying her eggs, we move the eggs to the hatchery to control the temperature and to protect them from predators and poachers."

"Are poachers a big problem?"

"It's a steady problem, I'm afraid. The turtle eggs have high protein content and our culture incorrectly considers them an aphrodisiac. Some of the restaurants around here will sell them on their menus or tourists will find them at road side stands. Some locals look at the eggs as a way to earn money or trade for drugs."

"Are they worth a lot of money?"

"It is rumored that a *huevero* can earn up to $1000 a night at $1.00 per egg. Last year we estimated $120,000 worth of eggs had been stolen."

"Aren't there laws against that?"

"There are, but they've only been enforced for the last couple of years and enforcement is random."

"That's awful. That's a large number of little turtles that won't make it to sea. We won't run into any of these hueveros will we?"

"Highly unlikely. They tend to hit the nests in the early morning hours, between our night and morning shift. A majority of turtles nest at night or early morning. We want to catch them as soon as they lay the eggs. A large percentage of the morning beach patrol consists of documentation from damaged and robbed nests, unfortunately."

They walked to the opposite end of the hatchery, "Let me share a little background on the turtles you'll work with. The leatherback is the only sea turtle that doesn't have a shell. They have an oily leather back with several bony plates that run lengthwise called a carapace. They're one of the largest living turtles. Growth can be up to seven feet and 2,000 pounds. The species dates back to the first sea turtle emergence 110 million years ago. They're actual living dinosaurs listed as critically endangered, being at the top of the sea turtle list."

"Wow. I had no idea they were that endangered. How did this happen?"

They walked to the shore's edge and sat in the sand. Laura watched the waves roll in and out as Gabriel continued his lesson.

"There are several ways. First, the turtle eggs feed some of the natural fauna in this area. Jaguars have been known to hunt and kill the female turtles. Coatis, raccoons, wild dogs, and birds try to get at the eggs for food. Fifty percent are caught by long-line fisherman, and they're also affected by coastal pollution like plastics, entanglement in abandoned nets or fishing equipment. Beach erosion around the world, new development on the beach, warmer ocean temperatures, and water level rise, due to climate change also affect nesting habitats and their food source."

A flock of small green parakeets flew from one end of the beach to the other. Laura's eyes followed and then she returned her attention to Gabriel.

"Our goal is to keep them in the hatchery until it's time for them to find their way back to sea. This will allow us to monitor the temperature of the nests, protect them from the natural predators and hueveros. It can take 45 to 60 days to become a hatchling."

"Will we find turtles every night, and how many eggs can they lay?" Laura relished all this new knowledge.

"May through July is peak nesting season on this beach, so we'll see an increase very soon. Each leatherback can lay 50 to90 eggs per clutch. Last year, we set a record of 1,500 eggs preserved. Each year the conservation programs get more support from volunteers, so that allows us to cover more ground and preserve more eggs. This is important because this beach hasn't been declared a national park. We hope that as volunteer interest grows it becomes more profitable for the locals to share the egg hatching events than to poach from it."

"Well then I'm glad I'm here to assist. The brochures LSTC sent me mention a variety of tasks that can be done. Can you explain how the beach patrols work?" Laura was willing to tackle any chore.

"Good question. With beach patrols, the crucial times are early morning before sunrise. We start about 4 a.m. and will go till dark, between 8 p.m. and through to 1a.m. The latter is when we want to find the nests. Beaches are deserted before the hueveros can make an impact. The early morning hours allow us to patrol the beaches for turtle tracks and the occasional mother turtle busy with her nest. She uses her flippers to dig the nest, lay her clutch, cover them, and then goes back to the sea."

A volunteer ran up to Gabriel. "Here are the tags you ordered. Just arrived."

"Thanks." Gabriel placed the small bag in his back pocket. "Where were we?"

"How many people work together on patrol?" Laura asked.

"Three, but that depends on the number of teams available. Each team takes a portion of the beach, usually a couple of kilometers."

"Why three?"

"Someone needs to make notes with the clipboard. If a large number of eggs were laid, all three will move them to bags or coolers to bring back to the hatchery. It takes two people to tag a turtle, if that needs to be done. Sometimes turtles need help with the digging or getting back to sea. I need to warn you, they can be quite large. Patrol teams also keep the beaches clean of trash and plastic bags.

"Why plastic bags?"

"Plastics in water resemble jellies, the turtle's favorite food, and if swallowed, will suffocate the turtle as they're not able to regurgitate."

Laura's mouth fell open, "Oh my God. That's awful. I've never thought of that, but you're right. They do look like jellies."

"People don't realize leatherbacks help control the jelly population by feeding on them. This affects the entire ocean eco-system. This simple process affects the amount of seafood available for people to eat."

"I had no idea."

"I'm sorry. I got sidetracked. You asked about the shifts. We'll have support from the policía spread out among the 18 kilometers of beach at night. They'll be in patrol cars along that road that breaks the beach with the trees." Gabriel pointed. "They look for unusual activity. Hueveros hide in the trees and watch for opportunity. We also have to guard the hatchery from theft, so we keep someone here at all times."

"You mentioned the misconceptions the local population have. Is there a program to inform them about the importance of the sea turtles?" Laura's mind began making lists of things she could help with.

"We do include locals in the volunteer program and hope that through word of mouth, they understand the importance of our conservation efforts. But when you're poor and hungry, your only priority is to meet basic needs."

"What can I do to start?" Laura stood tall, chest out, at attention.

"Bianca will be your mentor this week. Bianca," Gabriel called for her.

Bianca stopped what she was doing and joined them. "Show Laura how we have the rows and columns set up. You'll dig a preservation area and aid in the documentation needed. I need to go follow up with the other volunteers that have moved some deadwood in the area," Gabriel headed out.

Her volunteer days were now underway. Laura grabbed a pair of latex gloves and started to work in the sand. She turned to Bianca who kneeled next to her, "Did you know Gabriel before this trip?"

"I've only known him since I arrived here. I do know that Gabriel and Daniela have worked together for years."

"How did the Leatherback Sea Turtle Conservancy get started?" Laura asked.

"Daniela told me that Gabriel's grandfather worked with her father to create the LSTC. Gabriel's family lives near Cahuita, which is closer to the Panama border, but Gabriel spends most of his time on Playa Soledad. I think he is always very serious. We will need to include him in some fun. I know that he scuba dives and loves to talk about the beaches with the people he works with.

When you get a chance to work with him, ask him about those interests and you'll get to know him better."

"He gives the impression that he's quite passionate about what he does, but he seems lonely, too."

Chapter 5

Gabriel had given direction to three teams of volunteers on the last shift of the night and jumped into his gray Hyundai Tucson for his patrols. Halfway to the north shore, his vehicle lights spotted a couple of men he didn't recognize. Both were in their twenties, slim, wearing jeans and loose jersey tees. They used the turtle safe flashlights reserved for his group. He stopped to approach the men. "Hey, what are you doing?"

Juan Carlos and Luis turned to look at Gabriel.

"We're looking for turtle eggs," Juan Carlos said.

"I don't recognize you as part of our volunteer program. I'm Gabriel Montenegro with LSTC."

"We know. We watch you and your group," Luis said.

Gabriel saw how disheveled they looked, their eyes glassy. One of the men had an "S" shaped tattoo on his left arm, the other had a large burlap sack he suspected had eggs in it.

"How do you know about my hatchery? I haven't seen you around here before. I didn't realize there was another group on this beach," Gabriel said.

"Locals talk. Like I said, we watch you and your group, we know everything about you," Juan Carlos said.

"Do you have eggs in that sack?"

"Sí, we've been on patrol."

"Will you sell them?"

"Maybe. Will you buy them?"

"I'll pay you for that sack of eggs if you bring them to the hatchery, and promise to leave this beach. It's very important that we save those eggs. I'll have my security detail come get you. If you want to be volunteers then we need to get you registered with the program, otherwise you could be arrested for poaching." Gabriel dialed one of the security officers scheduled that night.

"I have a couple of guys I need you to pick up. They'll turn in a sack of eggs, and are not to return unless they've registered with our program." Gabriel gave Manuel a brief description of the men and their location and waited until Manuel's car arrived before he moved on to the northern point of Playa Soledad. Gabriel pulled in there as the volunteers on that stretch made their way back to their vehicles.

He sat on the beach to reflect. There were new faces he didn't recognize and he was certain they were hueveros. The thought that someone watched him and his group unsettled him as he remembered the threats on his life a year ago. *Lord, please watch over this beach and the safety of our volunteers* Gabriel prayed. He would call Daniela in the morning.

Gabriel got up to leave when a glimmer caught his eye. He moved to the water's edge to see what it might be. The moon reflected off of something, the spot of light bobbed up and down. There wasn't a buoy in the area. Was it a boat? He waded into the shallow surf to get a better look. *It's too late for fishing boats to be in the area.* The comment, "We watch you," replayed in his mind. He thought back to the previous year, the balaclava clad person on a motorcycle with the assault rifle pointed at him. *Please not again, Lord, we have good work to do here.*

Chapter 6

The dawn shift allowed Laura to watch incredible sunrises over the Caribbean. Soft pastel pinks, yellows, and pale blues stretched like thin cotton candy strands along the skyline. They reminded her of times at the fair.

Laura picked up a fishy smell then heard the heavy breaths of a mother turtle ready to lay her eggs. "Bianca, Gabriel, come see this." Laura said as she attempted not to disturb the turtle. She watched the female turtle drop her eggs one by one into the nest. Laura noted date, time, and location on the clipboard. Bianca focused her camera, "She is colossal. I've never seen anything so large."

"I feel like I've just watched history being made. This turtle could be older than all of our ages combined. Wow." Laura grabbed her waterproof camera from her pocket to document the moment.

"Wait till you see 'em hatch and move back to the sea." Gabriel replied as he moved to help the turtle. "Looks like she's in trouble with her right flipper, she might be stuck. I'll try to help her." With his headlamp on, he dusted the sand off her back.

"You didn't kid when you said they were large. This turtle is about as long as you are tall. Incredible." Laura squatted closer, her hands in the gritty, sticky sand as she watched Gabriel interact with the turtle. "I'm really glad I shifted to these early hours."

"Laura, do you have a tag available? This one hasn't been tagged. Bianca, come over by me, I'll need your help."

Laura slapped the sand from her hands onto her denim shorts, and reached in her pocket for a tag, noted the number on the clipboard and handed it to Gabriel.

"Laura, you're in my way, didn't you hear Gabriel ask for me?" Bianca pushed Laura to get by.

The mornings were dark, quiet, and the light breeze was always relief. She could tell the sun was about to rise when the sound of the birds began. It took her a couple of days to adjust to the turtle-safe red-tinted flash light, but as she acclimated, she realized her senses had become stronger with limited sight.

The turtle finished with her eggs and Gabriel helped guide her so she could make the slow awkward progression back to sea. The women gathered several soft white leather-like billiard ball sized round eggs into two bags and made their way back to the hatchery without conversation. Laura held her bag with care so as to not break any of the eggs and was relieved to make it the hatchery without incident. Now that they were in May, the nesting activity had increased. They expected a busy month.

***

"Esteban, it's Manuel. I have some information for you. Juan Carlos and Luis were confronted by Gabriel last night. Gabriel called me to make sure the eggs the two found were brought to the hatchery. He offered $100 for them and they took it. They want to know if they can keep the money since they felt it better to cooperate. They did tell him that they watched the beach and the volunteers."

"It's good they cooperated. We don't want the biologist suspicious. They probably earned more from him that night than they would have otherwise. This incident is really small change compared to the rest of the delivery. Let them keep the money, but be sure they are ready and alert for the next shipment."

Manuel headed to the ranch to give the news to Luis and Juan Carlos, but warned them to get permission from Beni or Esteban before they tried that stunt again. The two men were excited about their bounty and made plans to spend it.

Luis attached his beloved machete and sheath to his belt and pulled the belt tight so his dark jeans would stay at his waist. His dark fitted t-shirt was emblazoned with the emblem of his favorite soccer team. "Can you believe we've been at Pocora a week already? And we can use Esteban's motor bike when there's no shipments. We can get to the beach and get more eggs."

"Even better, he paid us for the turtle eggs we gathered and the crack we made. This stuff is great. I didn't know cooking was so easy." Juan Carlos laced his black boots.

"Did you grab a couple of rocks and the pipe? I'll need more energy tonight. Do you think it will help this headache?" Luis pushed back the stringy black hair that had fallen into his eyes.

"I'm glad Beni told us to go after midnight. We don't have to run into that biologist again, it's much quieter and easier to get the eggs. I feel like Superman on this stuff. I think I could run the entire beach and not get tired." Juan Carlos inhaled the pipe deeply and held his breath.

Luis's latest hit took effect as he spotted a couple of hueveros in their territory and charged at them with his machete. He just missed the arm of one of the hueveros but got close enough to nick the skin.

"¿Estás jodidamente locos?" the overweight huevero screamed. "¿Cual es tu problema?"

"My problem is that you are on my beach." Luis said as his dilated pupils stared the guy down.

"Man you crazy! You can have the damn beach, we'll go elsewhere. Come on, let's leave these idiotas."

"That was a rush." Luis and Juan Carlos laughed at the running men.

"This job is so much better than working the ports. Who knew we could find free food, a place to sleep, and drugs. Clemente should see us now, his loss that he fired us, hombre estupido."

"Let's move south and see if we can scare anyone else," said Juan Carlos.

Chapter 7

A couple of days later, Esteban had gathered his men at the Pocora ranch to prepare them for a new shipment. "We expect another delivery early Thursday morning at 1 a.m. Beni and Manuel you'll be out in the water to meet the fishing boat from Colombia. Meet them outside the Costa Rican boundary waters and transfer the shipment to the panga.

"Juan Carlos and Luis, you'll wait on the beach to help unload the packages into Beni's van.

"Manuel you'll be dropped off at shore to assist Juan Carlos and Luis once the packages are transferred, while Beni brings the boat back to the port near Tortuguero. The three of you will use his van to pick him up. Then head back to the ranch."

Esteban turned to Beni, "Our overhead is higher on this one because we contracted with an established and trustworthy fishing crew from Colombia that Wendigo hired. There's also an increase in fuel costs. This will be a 400 kilo shipment. I need you to cut this to 60 percent purity so we can make up some of the costs."

Wendigo's plan was to net a six-million-dollar profit from this. They had been fortunate to date in the timing of shipments. Other smugglers goods had been seized by the U.S. Navy, but Wendigo's got through.

***

Deadwood was stacked into a cone in a central area between the surf and the sandy road that separated the jungle from the beach. The pile was lit with blue and lavender flames that reached the sky while sparks danced and cracked in the darkness. The moonlight showed through in random swirls between cloud cover. Gabriel walked the north shore by himself, at about 10 p.m. He picked up on the smell of smoke and came upon a small group around the bonfire. He recognized Orlando Araya Lopez among the men.

Orlando was a huevero who Gabriel knew for the last couple of years and he had negotiated a partial save on some of the eggs from Orlando's take. He stopped to chat, "Hi Orlando, what's up?"

"It's the season for business to increase, my friend. This year, it seems there is more competition on this beach. Some of my buddies have reported that there is another gang, this one not afraid to threaten the others. One of them reportedly carries a machete with him," Orlando said.

"I ran into a couple of new guys the other night and the volunteers have reported more vandalism recently too."

"We know there's been fewer patrols this season with both the volunteers and the policía. Better for us. Would you like to join us? We have a bottle of *Centenario*?" Orlando held it out to Gabriel.

"No, gracías. I'll stick with my plans and hope to save more turtle eggs than you'll be able to find tonight. Just enjoy yourself."

"You shouldn't walk alone Gabriel. I don't like what I've heard about this other gang."

"Thank you for the warning. I'm almost done for the night." Gabriel waved at the group and walked away.

Orlando and his friends continued to drink. Eventually a drunken Orlando stumbled his way into the jungle's edge, tripped and passed out.

***

They had to work quickly. They only had a two-hour window before chances of being caught in the act increased. The panga made its way to the anchored fishing boat.

Manuel was off duty from the policía and on his side job as the security beach patrol communication link for Esteban. He also assisted with shipments. He only made the equivalent of $328 a month with the policía and was open to other opportunities to earn cash. Manuel and Beni quickly worked to unload the cocaine bricks from the fishing boat to the panga. Their goal was to get the shipment on the road by 4 a.m. before the annoying volunteers started back on patrols.

The pre-dawn hours were void of activity and the blackened sky offered enough cloud cover to keep the beach surroundings dark. Luis and Juan Carlos were unsupervised.

"I can't wait to see the semi-finals for Limón Futbal club. Do you think Esteban will give us the night off to come into Limón to watch it? Limón's had its best year yet," Juan Carlos asked Luis. He was taller than Luis, lighter complexioned with grey eyes that slightly bulged from the sockets. He wore dark jeans and a solid dark grey t-shirt that blended into the night.

"I hope so. I expect a close game. We should watch it at El Cevichito, I bet they'll have a big crowd," Luis replied as he pointed. "Look. There. We have ourselves a mamma turtle."

Juan Carlos turned to see a black leatherback with miniature milky white dots throughout her body. She was in the nest build process.

"Watch this. I'll carve out those eggs with my machete," Luis said. "Let's try to push her over onto her side. I'm gonna guess her weight will be too much for just one of us."

Juan Carlos blocked the turtle's movement, and stepped to Luis's side. They bent over her and tried to push, but could not roll her. Her left flipper moved in an agitated motion and almost hit Juan Carlos on the side of his head.

"She's heavy, has to be more than 150 kilos," Juan Carlos groaned. "She'll knock me out if that flipper hits me. This won't work we need more help. There's too much sand under her to get any leverage. Let's just take the eggs after she leaves them. Consider it extra pay while we wait for Manuel."

Juan Carlos ran to the van to grab some sacks. Luis walked in circles trying to figure out a way to cut open the turtle. She was just too big. They'd waited for her to lay the eggs and then collected them. Juan Carlos carried the bags back to the van while Luis raised his machete. It took him a while, a lot of strength, but blood spattered everywhere when he decapitated it.

"What have you done?" Juan Carlos returned, "how are you going to hide that?"

"Don't have to. No one will connect this to us. She was alive when we left with the eggs."

"Your machete. You better clean it before Manuel sees it."

What Luis and Juan Carlos hadn't seen was another huevero at the jungle's edge who heard their noise and witnessed the kill.

Chapter 8

Beni brought the panga and Manuel close to shore so he could jump out and catch up with the others. "What have you two been up to while Beni and I collected the shipment?" Manuel asked because he didn't trust them.

"We caught a couple of other hueveros who killed a turtle. I scared them with my machete and Juan Carlos grabbed the eggs." Luis fiddled with his machete sheath.

"Why don't I believe you?" Manuel stood rigid with anger on his face. "*¿Qué coño estabas pensando?*" I thought you'd been warned about threats to others on the beach. That biologist might suspect things other than poaching. We don't need to give him any proof that can be used in an investigation. We've been lucky that my brothers at the policía haven't enforced the poaching laws. Now is not the time to give them a reason to start. We have several more runs scheduled this month, and we must be ghostlike in our actions to not create suspicions. Let's get this van loaded, we need to pick up Beni at Port Soledad and get on the road."

***

Esteban's cell phone rang. "Yeah."

"It's Manuel. The package has been delivered. All seems to have gone smoothly, but Luis and Juan Carlos were a little careless tonight. I've warned them, but if it happens again, action may need to be taken to scare one or both."

"*Idiotas de mierda.* Tighten the leash on them and keep me posted."

***

At Brisas De La Playa, Gabriel sat alone on the patio, face toward the ocean in thought. His encounter with Orlando and the things he thought he saw replayed in his mind. He was angry. He called Daniela, "The Policía Nacional in Limón are not effective. They don't care that beach violence increased this year. What is the Ministry of the Environment doing? Even their actions are stalled."

"I'm doing the best I can Gabriel. I continue to push the minister and the *Organismo de Investigacíon Judicial* to get the local authorities to enforce the laws. They still use the excuse of budget cuts; it was much easier to get support last year," Her voice was tense with frustration.

"We've accomplished so much good in the last couple of years, why is this year so hard? What has changed? We had the support last year," he reminded her.

"Don't forget we had a similar problem. The local volunteers were tied up, threatened with knives and assault weapons. The hueveros were able to rob them of their belongings and took over 1,000 eggs. There was the assault and threat on Alma if she was seen on that beach again," Daniela typed more notes onto the laptop.

"We had more guards and the guards had more fire power than they do now. Why such a big change? I'd guess someone's palms are getting greased, if it has anything to do with budgets. I'll just need to get bolder." Gabriel would not frighten easily. This was his beach, all those years of work. The locals knew him and his reputation as a sincere person—certainly if he rallied his fans, they would help.

"Gabriel be careful. There's rumors of a new gang and if what we're hearing is true, I don't want you or your volunteers to get hurt."

"I think I'll call *La Nación*. Maybe I can get an interview and have the reporter spend an evening on turtle patrol. A news story will help the local *Ticos* add pressure to the government for increased security on Playa Soledad." He'd do anything.

"It's worth a try. We have nothing to lose, and the more attention we can bring on this subject to the public, the more support we can gain." Daniela concluded the call.

***

Luis and Juan Carlos didn't understand why Manuel was angry with them. They thought they said the right thing. They collected eggs and helped with the drug drop that was what they were hired to do. Juan Carlos came up with a new idea and shared it with Luis. "I have an idea. We can show Manuel and Esteban how we can help them. We can start to follow that biologist and those ladies that work with him. We can watch what they do when they're not on the beach and watch them from the trees when they are. We'll scare them and then they'll go home and leave the beach to us."

"I don't know," Luis scratched his forehead. "Manuel told us to act like ghosts. I got carried away with the turtle the other night. We don't need to make another big mistake. Besides, where will we find the time? We need to be alert for the beach at night."

"That's what the crack is for, man. We just keep smoking that and we won't need to sleep. We can do it. No one needs to know, not until we have something good to report. What harm can it do? I'll follow the *rubio*. You can follow the *pelirrojo*. I think these two are the leaders. They'll never see us."

"How would we follow them?" Luis scratched his arms. Had he picked up bugs?

"We watch from the trees when they're on the beach in the early morning. Esteban gave us that old blue and white motorbike to use to go between the ranch and Limón. I bet we can steal another one in town, and then you'll have one to use. The volunteers stay together most of the day. It'll be easy enough to follow them when they're separated."

***

The DJ played a salsa set as Bianca and Laura attempted the correct steps. They had enjoyed the groups day trip to the white sandy beaches of Cahuita where they heard the faint sounds of reggae music. They had cajoled Gabriel into an evening of drinking and dancing at Mercury, a discotheque inside one of the local hotels. They enjoyed the mix of salsa, reggae, and even pop music from the U.S. and Britain. "I love this music, what a great mix of songs." Bianca swayed her hips to the music at the bar. The

31

ladies noticed Gabriel only occasionally had a beer. To their surprise he was also quite the Latin dancer.

"Gabriel, you've been holding out on us. We had no idea you were a dancer too," Laura said.

"Lots of family celebrations. I learned young. We also learn traditional dances in school for festivals," he lifted the beer to his lips. "Who wants to learn the Merengue?"

"I do," Laura said

"Me too," Bianca chimed.

"I'll teach you both. Laura let's start with this song."

He demonstrated the steps, "It's a slower beat so we can begin by counting the steps. Merengue music usually gets pretty fast paced so it can get difficult the faster you move." Laura was ready to try. She picked up the steps quickly as they moved to *"Noche De Fantasia"* by Joseph Fonseca. Bianca was cheering and laughing at them until she took her turn. Juan Carlos watched them from a corner. Bianca danced with Gabriel, while Juan Carlos approached Laura. *"Yo quiero bailar contigo,"* he said. This guy looked younger than her, very casual, thin, and in need of a bath. She was a little apprehensive but didn't want to be rude. *"Seguro,"* she responded. He was a little out of sync with the beat but she politely danced as she motioned for her friends to come save her.

Chapter 9

Diamond sparkles of moonlight reflected off the water just before first light. This day, Laura and Bianca walked the beach patrol with a new volunteer, Anna Matthews. Anna was a recent college graduate out of Texas, with a firm muscular body and bouncy step that reminded Laura of a cheerleader she had known in high school.

"Hi Anna, I'm Laura. I'm your mentor for this new adventure. What brings you to Costa Rica?" She reached to shake hands.

"My parents thought I should become responsible after my college graduation. They think all I do is party. I just don't have a specific career interest. It's really not a big deal," a grumpy Anna said as she kicked the toe of her sneaker in the sand. "Who decided I get to start this job so early anyway?"

Laura rolled her eyes at Bianca, then turned to address Anna. "That would be Daniela the conservancy director. Believe it or not, you'll soon find this is one of the best shifts. Cooler temperatures, quiet mornings, I'm sure you'll come to enjoy it." Laura glanced at the clipboard of orientation notes.

They were assigned the northern stretch. After walking for 15 minutes, Anna saw something large in the sand and screamed. "Laura, over here. Come quickly." She'd found a decapitated turtle and its fluids congealed in the sand where the head should have been. "Oh my God. The poor thing, who could be so cruel. I think I'll be sick." Anna headed for the bank of trees to vomit.

"I need to call Gabriel. I've never seen anything like this. Why would someone do this to an innocent turtle?" said Laura. "I better get some pictures for documentation, don't touch or move a thing." She put in a call to Gabriel.

"I'll get the SUV, and be there in 10 minutes. I need to grab a couple of other people so we can move it before it starts to decompose," he said.

It's peak season and we had similar activity to last year, he thought to himself.

"There's quite a stench, a gross mess from fluids and blood. Flies are gathering. I've taken pictures, what else should we do?" Laura pinched her nose so she wouldn't get sick herself.

"Look around and see if you can find any other clues to how this happened. We don't have the facilities to do a necropsy, so we'll have to get the carcass back out to sea as soon as possible. I'll put in a call to the port and see if someone can bring a panga and tow rope to get it away from the surf."

As Laura walked the area, she used her little camera to take pictures of shoeprints she found. *They're too big to be Anna's, or ours.* She squatted closer and took more pictures.

Just a few feet away, Bianca found shoe prints that seemed to end at the undergrowth that lead to the thick of trees. "Hueveros," Bianca said, "More shoe prints over here, bring that camera."

Laura continued to walk north of where they found the turtle remains. A few yards ahead she called out, "Hey guys, over here. More shoeprints. These look like they lead to and from the water. They're above the high tide mark" called Laura. "Do you think someone came in on a boat to do this?"

Her stomach turned at the thought that someone would do this in cold blood just to steal eggs. Gabriel had alluded to poaching for drugs in her orientation, was this one of those cases? A chill ran up along her spine. To hear about the possibility of drugs was one thing, but another to stand in a location where it might have happened. They had discovered two more nests also robbed along their route that morning. Saving baby sea turtles wouldn't be as easy as she once thought.

***

Gabriel finally arrived, and Laura walked him through what they had seen and assured him she had taken pictures for review later. He was sure that the foot prints near the water signified drug smugglers in the area, and wondered if what he'd seen the other night was related.

There had been recent reports in the media of previous drug busts from Colombia and Panama off the shores of Playa Soledad. He had suspected for some time that drug smugglers used the north part of the beach as a drop off point. Media also suggested locals in the area were involved. Drug runners had been using an area between Limón and Tortugero as a distribution point and shipped drugs to Guapiles where they were held before being transported to the central valley and on into Mexico. The Costa Rican Government had removed their Coast Guard from shore patrol the previous year. It would be up to the United States and the Joint Maritime Agreement between the countries, to patrol the area and make the drug busts.

**

Despite the headache that throbbed from his overconsumption of rum the night before, Orlando acted out of character. He sought out Gabriel. "I need to speak with you," he said as he approached the hatchery.

"Sure, what is it? It's not like you to be spotted in daylight here," Gabriel said.

"Last night, after we spoke, I had stumbled into the jungle, tripped and must have passed out. Voices woke me. I watched through the trees. The guy with the machete I told you about, I saw him. He took that machete to the turtle. They took her eggs, and left her there."

"Three of my volunteers found those remains and called me. I saw the turtle. Were you able to get a look at their faces? Have you seen them before?"

"No, I'm afraid my head was a little fuzzy. When I saw the machete, I decided to lay low behind the trees and stay quiet. It sounded like they were having fun. I didn't want them to come get me. They seemed to be about my height, thin, maybe. I couldn't tell in the dark. A third man had come from the water towards them, then they moved away and I couldn't see them anymore. I stayed in the jungle afraid to move until I heard someone scream and then I ran further in."

"You did the right thing. I'm glad you told me about this." Gabriel made notes on a clipboard.

"I'm afraid the only job I know has very scary competition. I don't feel safe on this beach at night knowing someone has a machete, and they threaten to use it on people. Gabriel, give up the night shifts. They'll hurt you. They're dangerous people."

"I won't let them scare me. I'll go to the policía and ask for more help. I'll tell the policía I have a witness."

"You can't let them know it's me. They'll want to arrest me for poaching. You'd be handing me over to them." Orlando balled his fists.

"I won't give your name, I'll just say that a witness came forward," Gabriel tried to reassure.

Dismayed by the new activity and feeling at a loss on how to get more help, Gabriel used his Facebook page to encourage his followers to put pressure on the policía. He was so bold, he mentioned his thoughts on drug smuggling being involved. He hoped the added drama of the machete and the decapitated turtle would increase the urgency of the people to pressure the policía.

Chapter 10

A couple of nights later, Gabriel, Daniela, and a reporter from *"La Nación"* met on the beach around 11 p.m.

"Thank you for your time tonight and showing me what these patrols are all about. I'd like to include this and the history and purpose of LSTC in my article," said the reporter. Gabriel opened the passenger door of his car for the man.

"We had also invited a representative from the policía but they declined, said they didn't have enough staff. We're frustrated with the lack of support from the local authorities to help us save these eggs. We feel the policía and MINAE are not taking our requests seriously. This has not been a fair fight," said Gabriel.

Daniela told the reporter what to expect on the patrol as they headed out. She also explained the myth of the aphrodisiac. The reporter said he'd heard that, "Even though study after study have proven that myth false. By the way, I want to let you know that I also invited the policía to tour with us. They told me they didn't have the staff but were trying to support your group as much as possible."

"Well, they lie!" Gabriel interrupted. A few minutes later he stopped the vehicle.

"Look! over there." Gabriel pointed, "That is our first turtle for the night. She is already headed back to the water, so the eggs must be nearby." As they got out to look, they discovered the nest had been robbed. "The hueveros must be close, this happened very recently. They must be in the trees." Gabriel scanned the are in hopes the culprits would be spotted.

They moved back to the vehicle and continued on. They were out till 2 a.m. and the reporter made note that there had been no security patrol in those areas while they were out.

He asked Gabriel, "Aren't you afraid these night patrols? knowing these hueveros may only be a step ahead of you or hiding nearby?"

Gabriel shrugged, "Sometimes, but everyone on this beach knows me and my reputation as the person that saves leatherback turtle eggs."

They saved 100 eggs from two of the three nests they came upon. "Thank you for your time and this experience," said the reporter.

"Thank you for your interest. When should we expect to see your report in print?" Daniela asked.

"It should be out in a couple of days," the man said.

***

After her shift, Laura decided to jog through town before the expected late afternoon downpour hit. Change of scenery. She enjoyed the run through Limón to the port, brief break at Parque Vargas and then back to the Valverdes home. She was grateful for the time alone with her thoughts and to observe the Ticos going about their day. Today's visit into town was different; *Is that small blue and white motorcycle following me?* She turned. It turned and stopped just short of her destination. After what she had reported to Gabriel, she now wondered if she was followed or just paranoid. *I need to pay more attention to my surroundings, the color of that bike, and the size of the person riding it. Safety First,* repeating to herself a motto she had learned at work. She felt anxiety increase within her.

***

The volunteer group from LSTC looked forward to another social event. This time, a zip line canopy tour at Gandoca-Manzanillo National Wildlife Refuge close to the Panama border. Laura used this opportunity to speak with the others on the bus to compare notes about the hueveros and if they'd observed any suspicisous activity lately.

"I've seen damaged nests on my new night shift also. And, now that you mentioned it, I think I have been followed. Really skinny, dirty looking young guy. I've seen him around the mercado and the lavandaría just this past week. I just thought it a coincidence," Bianca told her. "I figured I only paid attention to it because of Gabriel's warning." Bianca and Laura promised they'd watch their surroundings more closely and compare notes.

Laura approached Daniela next and wanted to know more about the history of the program. "My father started this program. Gabriel and I used to patrol the beaches together a couple of years back. I took over the program just this year when my father became ill. That's one of the reasons I spend more time in San José than in Limón Province."

"Did you experience vandalism and poaching then?" asked Laura.

"Sí, I'm afraid so. The activity seems to pick up in correlation to the increase in turtle nesting. The turtles are protected by the Federal Endangered Species Act, but unfortunately that isn't always enforced and not in all areas. I've decided to make LSTC headquarters in San José so I'm better able to work with the Costa Rican government through MINAE and the Ministry of Public Security. As a matter of fact, I've been pushing the ministries to increase funding of local police for security patrols. MINAE hasn't been very responsive. I make appointments and then they get cancelled by the minister." Daniela glanced out the window, then turned back to Laura.

"Gabriel tells me he is seeing new faces and others have given him feedback about a new group this year." Daniela's voice turned grave. "Continue to give reports to Gabriel as necessary and document the damage or robberies and locations that you come across. He'll communicate the escalation of poaching events to me, and I'll do my best to set meetings with MINAE, MSP and OIJ for law enforcement."

"What else we can do?" Laura was worried. "It's a shame we can't cover the entire beach to protect new nests."

"I understand everyone is doing the best they can. Unfortunately, we have a few more challenges this year than we faced last year. The good news is the conservation community is getting stronger. The community is working globally to send funding where necessary. We have a few rallies planned in San José to push MINAE toward stricter action regarding poaching throughout Costa Rica," Daniela reached into her handbag for her lip balm.

Laura touched Daniela's arm. "Would it be possible to come with you sometime? I'd like to see how the system works. I wouldn't mind participating in a rally, if that'd help."

"We'll see. You only have a few weeks left before its time for you to go home."

"I feel more at home here than I do back in California. I'm surprised at how protective I've become over these turtles and this program. Trying to save hatchlings feels like the most productive thing I've been involved with in quite some time. Being in this environment, the diversity of landscape and the marine life, I feel like I'm remembering who I am. Many of the locals I've met are living with what I would consider the basic essentials and they're happy without all the stuff I thought I had to have in the states. This has helped me develop new priorities."

Laura sat back and watched the landscape move past her. She thought back to her hectic life. The constant fights with her ex-husband, how she learned about his gambling problem. She'd had to find an alternative to keep her money safe. Her parents urged her to divorce and she felt like a failure. Laura kept a stiff upper lip with demands and unreasonable deadlines at work, and learned the hard way, that life was too short to waste on negative things. She used to thrive in the corporate environment, but now she pushed it away. Was it because of the failed marriage, or was she just changing?

Chapter 11

The next day, Laura was at the lavandería and recognized the motorcycle she thought had been following her a couple of days ago.

She walked across the street to the internet café with her tablet to send emails to friends and family, and felt someone staring at her. If she got up to order a beverage, she could survey the area. As she arrived at the counter, Juan Carlos approached.

"*Eres muy Hermosa*," Juan Carlos said.

"Are you talking to me?" asked Laura

"*¿Sí, puedo comprar un café?*"

"Thank you for the offer, but I'm on my way out. Do I know you? You look familiar."

"Sí, we danced together once. You live with Clemente don't you?'

"How do you know that?" she asked as she stared at him hairs on her neck standing on end.

"I saw you running to his house one day. I worked for him until he let me and my friend go. Said there was no more work." He stared at her with his head tilted to the side. "I hope he is nicer to you."

"I hate to break up this conversation but I better be on my way."

Laura gathered her things, headed out the door back to the lavandaría, and dialed her cell phone. "Clemente, can you pick me up at the lavandaría? I just had the strangest encounter and don't feel comfortable walking home. I hope I'm not interrupting anything, but this guy just gave me the creeps."

"I'll be right there, hang on."

She hung up with Clemente and made another call. "Gabriel, I just had the oddest meeting. I was in the café across from the lavandaría. Do you remember that guy I told you I danced with at the disco? He was there. He came up to me and offered to buy me a coffee. He knows where I live. Clemente is coming to pick me up, but I'm definitely being followed," Laura said. "No, I didn't get his name. I just high tailed it out of there. What should I do?"

"You did the right thing calling Clemente and me. I'll let the policía know. Going forward, I don't want you to venture out alone, have a buddy with you."

***

Bianca left the Banco de Costa Rica on Calle 5 and headed south toward the Mercado Central on Market Street. The streets weren't busy, but she thought someone was following her on foot. She quickened her steps and hoped to lose him in the market. She made a left onto Market Street and noticed he headed in the same direction. *This is Market Street, many people have a reason to be here, you're being paranoid.* She ducked inside and stopped at the nearest stall. She took a side glance and saw a young, gaunt, dark skin, dark wavy haired man, who looked like a teenager. He was dressed in denim jeans and a light blue t-shirt. He had stopped at a stall two down from where she was. She continued down the row and made another left. She stopped at a fruit stand. There he was again, another two stalls to her left. She went to pay for a mango and saw him reach for something in another stall. There was a mark on his left forearm, dark, like an *S* from what she could tell. *He's just shopping.* She relaxed a little, and moved along. She looked for the eggs and some fruit pulp and needed a couple of postcards to send off to friends. She was in the mercado for about 30 minutes, and left in the same direction she came. She stopped to cross the street when she recognized the same kid behind her. Again, quickening her steps, she searched for a cab to take her back to her assigned residence. *He is being a bit obvious if he is following me*, she thought.

***

The volunteer trio had planned to enjoy an afternoon on the beach, until a riptide almost drowned Anna. She was shaken, but ok and rested on her beach towel. Laura scanned the beach toward the trees and hoped to find a shady spot. She was sure she saw the motorcycle again. "Hey, look," she pointed. "That's the motorcycle I keep seeing. I was accosted this morning at the lavandaría. Do you think they're connected?" she asked Bianca.

"I've seen that motor bike around here often. Are you sure it doesn't belong to one of the other volunteers?" Bianca leaned up on an elbow.

"I don't think so. I don't recall seeing anyone drive up in it."

"I can't be sure, but it seems similar to one I thought had followed me around town," Bianca said.

Laura stood up from the sand, dusting the accumulated granules from her backside and legs. "I've got that sun-beaten feeling. We should move up to the trees where we can get a little shade and Anna can rest a bit longer."

"If you say so," was the reply.

They had just laid out their beach towels, when Juan Carlos jumped out at them and waved Luis's machete. "You need to go back where you came from. Stop the patrols or someone's going to get hurt," he said as he pointed the machete at Laura. He was high, pupils dilated. "Let's get out of here. NOW!" Bianca yelled. They ran to their bikes and pedaled quickly back to the Valverde residence to call Daniela.

Daniela said, "Ladies, you have choices. If you are not comfortable working Playa Soledad we can relocate you to another area, near Cahuita for example, or you can go home if you prefer. The last thing I want is for someone to get hurt."

"I wanna go home. I never wanted to be here in the first place and I almost drowned today," Anna said. "I do have one request before I leave, though. I'd like to see a live turtle. Do you think that's possible in the next couple of days? I'd really like to leave by the end of the week."

"There's been more activity on the night shift then I've seen on the morning shift when I worked it. I bet Gabriel will let you do a couple of night shifts with us. Laura if you want to join us, we'd have a bigger group and we'll be safer in numbers," Bianca suggested.

"Maybe switching our routine will keep that guy from following us," Laura said.

Bianca called Gabriel, "We want to work the night shift with you for the next couple of nights. Anna has decided to leave the end of this week and she would really like to see a live turtle." She explained the situation they encountered at the beach.

"I don't know, I don't think that's a good idea," said Gabriel.

"We'll all be together. Four of us in a group would be safer, right? We'd take your SUV. You know where to find them and traveling by car will be faster than if we walked. We'd be able to leave faster if something did look out of place, and all five security guys will be there. What could possibly happen?" Bianca was insistent.

"Alright. just the next couple of nights. If we don't see anything than Anna will just have to accept that. How do I let you talk me into these things?"

***

Juan Carlos was bragging to Luis that he flirted with the blonde at the café and scared the women on the beach earlier. Luis told Juan Carlos to be quiet or he was going to get in trouble and ruin their chances of being part of the next shipment. Luis mentioned this to Beni, who mentioned it to Manuel, who called Esteban.

"Esteban, Juan Carlos is getting out of control and making decisions on his own. He's becoming a risk to the operation. He admitted he approached one of Gabriel's volunteers and threatened a couple of them on the beach earlier," Manuel said.

"I'll take care of Juan Carlos," Esteban said.

"That biologist has been posting more requests for security patrols on his Facebook page. *La Nación* did a report on patrol with him. This could increase the focus on the beach. Will that affect our shipments?"

"I meet with Wendigo tonight about that. I'll let him know of these developments. I believe this shipment will be the largest one so far.

"Find someone to replace Juan Carlos." Esteban ended the call and threw a glass against the wall *damn it, another crack head out of control.*

***

The next morning, Juan Carlos parked his motorcycle, and walked across Avenida 2 between Calle 3 and 4 to the Mercado Central for its daily opening. He didn't see the vehicle that hit him. He was dead by the time the *ambulancia* arrived.

Chapter 12

"Hola, mi compadre." Esteban slapped his friend on the back. He met his boss and long-time friend, Wendigo, at Casa Roja a lounge located in the central part of Puerto Limón. The typical dark, smoke filled, seedy little place that catered to men. One could watch poor quality porn movies on televisions placed throughout and listen to very loud Latin music that blasted from a nearby sound system. The heavy rainy evening was a perfect time for an inconspicuous meeting and cervezas. Wendigo was handsome, well groomed, with an athletic build, artic blue eyes, short cropped hair and a clean-shaven baby face. His style said he was raised in money. He had flown in on a private jet to check on business and banking. Esteban was grateful he was generous with the payroll.

"I wanted to meet so we can plan this next shipment, I think you may need a couple of extra men," Wendigo said as Esteban pulled his chair to the table.

"I have good news as well regarding Pacuare River Adventures. We've had a great *temporada turística* this year, and I have some expansion ideas I wanted to share," Esteban said.

Following a brief run through on the basics of the existing business Wendigo got serious. "How is Manuel working out in obtaining information from the beach patrols?"

"Very well. He reports in daily and let me know we had a junior member take a little too much initiative. Unfortunately, that member met with a fatal accident on his way to Mercado Central recently. We're working on a replacement."

"Good." Wendigo lit a cigar and continued. "We're going to need additional men along with yourself, and the others. I'll be picking up a yacht from my broker tomorrow and will have a shipment coming from Colombia in a couple of days. We'll need a panga boat with two men to meet mine off the North shore of

Playa Soledad. I'll have an inflatable raft with 500 kilos of the goods inside the chambers. One of the men will need to get into the inflatable to start the small motor and get it to shore. On shore, it will take at least four men to unload. Slice the inflatable open and get the stuff to the Pocora location quickly. Be sure to remove the pieces of the inflatable from the beach. You'll need to stow the engine; we may be able to use it again down the road. The drop is planned to take place on Wednesday around midnight. I realize this is a little earlier than the past shipments. Split the value of one kilo with the men. This shipment must be on deadline. I'll have a decoy inflatable to replace the one you'll be bringing ashore in case someone wants to inspect the boat. This is an eight-million-dollar investment, we can't afford any mistakes. If there are, it won't be traced back to me."

"I understand. I have a guy in mind already, another laid off from the ports and desperate for income. I'm sure we can find an additional body," said Esteban. "About the inflatables, I had an idea. I thought we could look at expansion into rentals through one of the hotels near the beach. Not only would that serve to increase revenue, but the inflatables wouldn't look out of place on the beach or in the water. I was thinking that would make a cover for future drops."

"I like that idea. We will need to explore the logistics. Let's get this shipment completed first. Now if you'll excuse me I have a plane waiting." Wendigo stood, shook Esteban's hand, dropped a wad of cash on the table, and left.

Esteban had glanced at the grainy porn throughout their conversation, and felt a strong desire to pick up a little local gal and discover her talents. He enjoyed the variety of prostitutes he could legally purchase while away on his business trips.

***

"Tomas, back to Baranquillo," Wendigo ordered his pilot to fly his Gulfstream G150 with the caramel colored leather seats to Panama to meet is yacht broker. "Yes, Sir. Anything to drink before we take off?" Tomas asked.

"A shot of *Aguardiente*."

The next morning, Wendigo took custody of a gently used 50' Viking Convertible. "I've had a custom boat hoist added to the bow per your request," said the broker. "This allows a heavy inflatable or jet-ski to be lifted onto the water easily. I think you will find her to be a beauty and quite comfortable. I'm confident it will suit your needs." *A perfect home away from home* Wendigo thought. Too bad he would only own it for a short time before changing to another option.

***

Wendigo enjoyed his lifestyle. He met his grandfather at the business office of his family's legitimate and quite successful children's apparel manufacturing business. They had several locations throughout Colombia. Wendigo was a third generation drug smuggler. "*Abuelo*, we are set to unload are biggest shipment into Costa Rica soon."

"I'm proud of you, you have learned patience, strategy and understand the risks of the smuggling business very well," his abuelo said. The family's strong support mechanism ran through Colombia and parts of Panama; the Herrera family were untouchable.

"We are pleased that you have extended our business throughout Costa Rica and into Mexico. You are the first generation to accomplish this growth. Were you able to succeed with your bribes to the Minister of Environment?" Bribing policeman, politicians, and drug enforcement agents was nothing new for the Herreras.

"Abuelo, you have taught me that money always speaks loudest. Yes, I have paid informants and supporters throughout the Costa Rican government." His charm worked as well in negotiating those deals as it did with women.

***

Esteban briefed his men the following morning at the rafting office. Manuel, Beni, Luis and the new guys Pedro, and Alonso were there for instructions and orders. He laid out the plan for the shipment scheduled Tuesday.

"I'll be borrowing a green tourist van which will get four of us to the beach without suspicion. Each of you will need to have your ski mask and loaded AK-47 at the ready in case the volunteers and Gabriel are in the area. The beach needs to be cleared and vehicles back to Playa Soledad by 11:45 p.m. at the latest."

"Will you be needing my van?" Beni asked

"Yes. You and Pedro will need to get to the port to get the panga by 10 p.m. Pedro, you'll need to bring the van to the beach immediately after dropping Beni. Beni, you'll wait with the panga off the northern shore of Playa Soledad to pick me up so we can meet Wendigo's yacht by midnight. Have your ski mask on and bring your gun for protection. Keep the lights off. "

"What if there are volunteers on the beach, then what?" Pedro asked

"We will contain the volunteers. It will be important to get them from behind and immobilize their arms immediately. Manuel, you'll hang back to watch the beach as it's your normal security patrol duty and we won't arouse suspicion. If you see Gabriel and the volunteers, give them a warning that you've seen suspicious activity and advise them to leave at once. You'll need to radio me ahead of time should anything look out of place."

"Understood," said Manuel.

"The shipment needs to be loaded into the van and on its way to Guapiles by 1 a.m. Our client has set a specific time for delivery that must be met. Each of you will earn $2,500 for the night's work. Any questions?" Everyone agreed they understood the plan. "We're running short on time. I'm counting on that fact that Gabriel is predictable and will be on the beach starting his turtle patrols by 9." Esteban glanced at each of the men.

"I owe you payment for the eggs you've gathered these past couple of weeks. I must commend you on a job well done. It seems we have cornered the market on the poaching business on Playa Soledad. Your strength and intimidation, and Luis, your machete, have successfully put a scare into the veteran hueveros. This strategy has aided our group controlling that north shore. As an additional reward for the groundwork laid there will also be an opportunity to purchase some goods after we get this shipment to the distribution point."

***

Luis was so excited about having an AK-47 in his possession he couldn't wait to post a photo of himself with it on his Facebook page. There he stood, bare-chested in his green and brown mini-plaid pajama pants, AK-47 in his hands smiling for the camera. He thought he looked every bit the tough guy he imagined he was.

Chapter 13

The women came into the hatchery as Gabriel finished a phone call.

"Gabriel, there were some suspicious characters on the north shore earlier tonight. I don't have backup. I would advise you to visit another part of the beach," Manuel said.

"I appreciate the report Manuel, but you said you saw them earlier so that sounds like they're gone now. The volunteers are here I have to go." He ended the call.

Anna only had a couple of nights left in Costa Rica, so she hoped tonight would be the night she saw a turtle lay eggs. Gabriel, wearing his headlamp, checked his clipboard for times and location of the latest deposits to the hatchery. "Looks like our best chance is start at the center section and move north if necessary. Let's go." He walked to his SUV, and opened the back door for the women to board. The north shore was chosen because the last turtle spotted had been there.

Thirty minutes later and nothing had been spotted except huevero vandalized nests. Bianca, in charge of documentation, made note. Gabriel parked and glanced into his rear view mirror. A green tourist bus pulled up but he didn't give it a second thought. They headed to the north sector where Gabriel recognized the tractor-tire like markings in the sand.

"Look, over there." Gabriel pointed to the tracks. "This looks promising, maybe she's just beyond the bend." Everyone leapt from the 4WD eager to see activity.

"I'm sure this is it. I can feel it. Something exciting is about to happen," Anna said. They flipped on their turtle-safe flashlights and proceeded with care towards the tracks. They rounded the bend and saw her. "Oh my God, she's huge," Anna said as she spotted the blue-black turtle with faded white blotches.

"I'm going to help dig this area for her. She'll be able to get into position quicker, and we can see the eggs sooner," Gabriel fell to his knees near her back flipper. Bianca and Laura measured her at six feet. "I don't think I'll ever get tired of seeing this," Laura said.

"She's so beautiful; these turtles really do look prehistoric." Bianca said as she aimed her camera lens. The process of waiting for the clutch of eggs was slow.

***

It was time for Esteban's gang to put their plan in motion. Those damn volunteers and Gabriel were still on the beach. They were going to have to force a stop to that and contain them to meet the delivery deadline. They donned their masks and grabbed their guns.

***

Gabriel and the women stood in a semi-circle watching over the turtle, their backs to the parking area. Esteban gave the signal. His men donned their ski-masks, slung their AK-47s over their shoulders and crept up behind them. Gabriel heard something and started to turn, but Esteban hit him in the stomach with the butt of the gun and watched him double over. His hands were tied and Manuel pulled a sack over his head. The others turned to see what happened, but by the time it registered, they too had someone on them from behind grabbing their arms in a bear hold. The men immobilized the volunteers while Manuel helped with more sacks and rope. The men were strong and forceful.

Alonso grabbed Laura and thought he had her until her elbow hit his chin. Now pissed off, he arched back and lifted her from the ground. She couldn't get her foot to kick a knee or stomp the inside of her attacker's foot. Manuel stepped in to drive a fist to her gut, and down she slumped, air leaving her. A sack was placed over her head and her arms bound behind her back.

The other women were kicking and screaming until Esteban's deep voice said "Shut up, or we'll shoot. There is no one around to hear you." Alonso dragged Laura and stuffed her into a vehicle. Someone with very rancid and heavy breath was far too close to her for comfort. She felt steel against her ribs and heard Gabriel plead with his captor as he, too, was shoved into the vehicle. Laura sat on the lap of her attacker, his long hair draped over her neck, his arms engulfed her, his heavy breathing filled her ears and she steeled herself from panic. *Oh my god, what is happening?*

Blinded and bound, Laura heard the noise of a second vehicle behind her. Her heart pounded in her chest and her breathing was shallow and frantic. *I must slow my breathing and think.* "Gabriel?" she asked as her captor tightened his hold. Alonso whispered, "Be quiet." She retched at the stench of his breath.

"I'm here. We'll be ok." Gabriel tried to reassure her as he licked blood from his lip. Where were her other friends? Were they in the other vehicle she heard? Trying to replay the events in her head, she thought that they must be in Gabriel's SUV as it seemed she was hauled in that direction. She realized the packed sand path become a smoother paved road under the tires. They had traveled for what felt like several minutes and then she felt the bumps and potholes in the road beneath her jostle her around, pushing her body back into her captor's.

Bianca and Anna had been dragged to the van and held at gunpoint by Luis and Pedro. *"Eres tan hermosa que te quiero"* Luis said into Anna's ear as he moved close to her moving his hands up her shirt.

"Stop. Leave me alone" Anna tried moving away and kicking him.

"Ah, a combatiente," Luis continued with taunts and sexual innuendos.

"Stop it," she screamed louder.

Pedro saw her move, and pushed the muzzle of his AK-47 into her stomach.

"Be quiet, do you want to get us killed?" Bianca asked.

It quieted to the noises from the van's engine, and Bianca's own heart racing, as she focused on listening to her surroundings trying to figure out where they were and what was happening.

***

The vehicle stopped. Laura remembered, in the brief confusion at the beach, that there were maybe three men ski-masked with large assault weapons in their hands. She was grabbed, her stomach still hurt from the punch, but that horrid breath moved away. She didn't understand what was going on, it had been a quiet and joyful night on Playa Soledad with her friends as they watched a mother turtle lay her eggs. She wondered if these men had been hiding in the stand of palm trees at paths end. She hadn't seen anything unusual. She racked her brain for anything she might remember.

"Where are we?" Laura asked.

"Shut up" was the reply.

Alonso pulled her out of the Tucson. She could hear her other friends nearby. She was pushed and dragged into a dilapidated wooden building.

Pedro grabbed Bianca. "Get out," he pushed and then dragged her from the van. Luis, high on a cocaine adrenaline elixir, felt powerful and dominant, stronger than he had ever remembered feeling. He took advantage of the moment alone with Anna and pushed her to the floor of the van. "Please don't, let me go," she resisted. He smacked her across her face and put his weight on top of her. She felt the sting through her head sack. Her hands tied behind her back told her she could only kick, but he was on her in such a way that she couldn't gain leverage. Her shoulders pinched underneath her. He pulled at her shorts lowering them and forced himself into her. He felt control. Power. Dominance was pleasure. *This can't be happening, it must be a nightmare,* Anna thought to herself.

Laura heard a scream. At the same time felt Bianca's body fall onto the floor next to her. She felt someone take her shoes. She was frisked. They took her camera and phone from her pocket. Had she dropped the flashlight?

"Anna." She couldn't see anything, could only feel the floor under her. "Bianca? Is that you? Are you ok? Did they hurt you?"

"I'm okay, bruised. What the fuck just happened?"

Laura heard something like tin hit against wood. She could hear her friend Gabriel pleading to be let go, "Please, you've made a mistake. Let us go. We don't know you, we won't tell anyone." He kept trying to dodge a large piece of wood, but they kept hitting him on his back with it. *What the hell is going? who are these men?* Esteban, short on temper, adrenaline flooding his veins and aware that the clock was ticking on the time to get back to the beach, used the butt of his gun again, this time to the back of Gabriel's head. Laura heard one last groan.

Anna, sobbed as she was thrown into the room with Laura and Bianca. The women moved closer to her hoping to comfort her with the closeness of their bodies. With tied hands, they couldn't reach out for each other.

"Anna, are you ok?" Laura asked.

"No. I've been raped. I can't believe I had to come to this god forsaken place." More sobs.

"Oh Anna, I'm sorry. I wish I could hug you." Laura fought back tears.

Alonso and Manuel crammed Gabriel in the back of his Tucson, the others climbed back into the van for the drive back to Playa Soledad. They were on schedule by a narrow margin.

Laura faintly heard vehicles drive away and everything became quiet. Motionless.

Chapter 14

The time had come to meet Wendigo. Esteban signaled Beni to pick him up with the panga, leaving the others waiting on the beach. With another adrenaline surge, Luis stripped Gabriel and tied him to the bumper of his SUV. Luis climbed into the driver's seat and dragged Gabriel's limp body along the beach for fun. The others were frozen into place. No one moved to prevent it.

When Luis stopped, Gabriel was barely breathing, his body scraped and blistered from the sand. Luis shoved sand down Gabriel's throat and pushed his head into the turtle nest he and the volunteers had stood by. Alonso and Pedro gathered the eggs left behind while Luis was occupied. Manuel paced back and forth *mierda, meirda, this wasn't supposed to happen. No one was supposed to get hurt. What do we do now? How will we hide the body from Esteban?* He heard the boat motor in the distance and gathered the men. They left Gabriel and went to help with the delivery.

***

The sack over Laura's head was stifling, perspiration from her forehead burned her eyes and she couldn't see a thing. She thought *if I focus on Anna and Bianca, I won't have to think about how I feel.* Anna continued to cry. "My nose is bleeding, He hit me. He attacked me. I think I'm going to be sick".

"Can anyone see anything?" asked Bianca.

"No" they replied in unison. All of their heads had been covered.

"It is really quiet. Do you think they left? Are we alone?" Bianca whispered struggling to free her wrists from the rope.

"I don't know. Do we just sit here or try to escape?" asked Laura.

"If we don't do anything, they might come back." said Bianca.

"I need to get out of here," Anna sounded panicked.

"The first thing we need to do is figure out how to get theses covers off our heads and untie each other," Laura wondered if men were guarding the door. She asked, "Did anyone see what happened?"

"I only heard your scream. Someone snuck up behind me and put a sack over my head. I tried to scream, I tried to kick, but I just hit air," Anna said.

"They had ski-masks and guns pointed at you and Gabriel," Bianca said. "I don't know why I didn't run. I don't think my brain figured out what was happening."

"Whoever they are, they've got Gabriel. There had to be at least four of them." Laura said. "I'm not sure if someone is on guard outside. We need to free ourselves. Let's try to use our shoulders and arms to remove these sacks. We can start with Anna. Bianca, you can get on the other side of her. If she bends over a little, we can use our shoulders to pull off the sacks."

"That's sounds like a dumb idea," Bianca's anxiety was increasing.

"Got a better one? We won't be able to assess our needs until we can get these off." Laura said.

"Please Bianca, get this thing off of me. I can't breathe. Do what she says," Anna pleaded.

Several minutes passed before they managed to get the hoods off and breath easier again. Everything had been taken, no tools, no phones, and pitch black inside the shed. They tried to help each other with the ropes but needed to find something to loosen or cut them.

"My wrists hurt, this rope digs into them every time I move and my shoulders are cramping," Anna whined.

"Can you both stand?" Bianca asked. "I have an idea. We each take a wall and walk slowly along it. Maybe we'll find something to cut these ropes. The room seems to be pretty small. Maybe we're in a storage shed."

"It's worth a shot," Laura said.

"Hey, there's a hole in the wall over here. I feel air coming in. I'll try to see if I can find something sharp we can use, maybe a piece of board." Bianca yelped. She bent toward the hole breathing in the air as if it would clean and recharge her. Nothing sharp.

Bianca tumbled back to the floor and yelled, "I tripped over something. It feels large, rubbery," She turned her back for a better grip. "It's flat and long."

"Is it something we can use?" asked Laura.

"It's too cumbersome for me to grab with my hands. I'll see what I can do using my feet and legs. It feels like one of those river rafts. I bet we're at one of those raft launches, somewhere northwest of Limón, maybe."

"Let's keep feeling around the walls and floors, maybe there are some tools we can use," Laura said.

It felt like hours passed and they weren't any farther along than when they got here.

Claustrophobia set in and Anna panicked. "I can't breathe, I can't see, I need to get out of here!"

"Anna! Focus on my voice. You need to slow your breathing. Breath with me," Laura coached, "Breath in 1. . . 2. . . 3, out 1. . . 2. . . 3, In 1. . . 2. . .3. . .4. Out 1. . .2. . .3. . .4." She counted steadily to calm Anna.

"For God sake Anna, quit being a cry baby. We are all in this together, we all want to get out of here," Bianca chided.

"Calling names isn't making this easier. We need to keep calm and work together." Laura said. "I haven't heard any sounds. I think we're alone. Lucky for us, they didn't bind our feet or legs. We're going have to walk out of here with our hands as they are."

Laura backed into what she hoped was a door latch. "It's not locked. I think I might be able to open it."

"What if we leave and fall getting out of here?" Anna asked.

"What would you rather do? We have to take a chance. If we fall, we get back up," Laura said. She opened it slowly, the dark rainforest surrounded them. They had little moonlight to navigate by. They huddled together, straining their night vision to see in front of them. Movement was slow. Deliberate. They listened for a possible ambush. They pushed forward in bare feet avoiding rocks, potholes, and the huge nocturnal beetles with long needle like protrusions coming from their heads. Laura saw a dead one once in a museum and hoped she wouldn't encounter one.

"Ow, I stubbed my toe," Anna said. "At the rate we're moving, it will be morning before we get anywhere."

"Whine, whine, whine. I've had it with you," Bianca said

"What are you going to do about it, bitch?" Anna responded.

"Knock it off. Neither of you is helping this situation." Laura said with authority.

"Who made you queen?" Bianca said.

"I'm just trying to get us out of this. Making enemies out of each other isn't helpful," said Laura.

They were all uncomfortable as they moved over rocks, gravel, and dirt. The size of the rocks changed underfoot. A deep growl echoed around them.

"Oh my God, what's that noise? We're going to be killed by a jaguar," Anna screamed.

"Anna, calm down and be quiet. It's just howler monkeys, you've heard them before," Laura reassured everyone. "They don't start calling until just before dawn. I'm guessing we were in that shack for at least four hours. I'm glad I used mosquito repellent earlier, but I think something just found my ankle and the top of my foot," Laura tried a joke to break the tension.

Their fears ebbed the further they walked. The shack was on a pathway they were able to follow to a crossing.

"We must be at Route 32," said Bianca. "This will be paved and more even to walk on. I say we go left."

"I hope you're right, otherwise we have a long walk to nothing," Anna added.

The night was eerily silent. "I'm sure the ocean is in this direction, it will take us back to Limón, but we still have a long walk ahead of us," said Bianca.

***

Esteban and Beni rendezvoused with Wendigo in the nick of time. Wendigo had already used the hoist on the yacht and the inflatable was in the water waiting. Esteban got in the inflatable and took charge of getting it to shore. Wendigo had replaced the inflatable with a decoy on deck and was preparing to cruise towards the Caymans.

It pulled up on the beach, and the crew was ready to cut into it and get the product out of the chambers. They worked in unison to unload a chain of sausage-like casings full of cocaine from the inflatable to Beni's van. "We'll need to be sure we've gotten all the sections of the raft," Pedro ordered. "Stuff them in the back of the tourist van and I'll dispose of them when I return it. Put the motor in there too and I'll get that put into storage." Everyone else would be headed to Guapiles. They were so caught up in getting the shipment to the distribution point on time that they forgot Gabriel was lying near his vehicle. Esteban never saw him.

***

Several hours of hiking left their feet burned and their hands and arms numb behind their backs. They made it to a house at the edge of Liverpool, just west of Limón. They weren't sure they could've walked any further.

"Look. That house up ahead has a porch light on. I hope someone's home," Bianca said.

"I think we're about to find out." Laura said.

They knocked on the door and after a brief wait a man answered. They had woken him from sleep.

"Can you please help us? Call the *policía* we were kidnapped!" Bianca pleaded in Spanish to the man.

He cut the ropes and circulation returned to their arms, guzzling the water he gave them. With a place to rest, ice for their rope burns, and cold, wet towels for their wrists and faces, no one realized that they might be removing evidence. They just wanted to remove the night. They still had to wait for the police and someone to bring them home.

Anna's nose had been bloodied, but she was able to clean it up.

Laura tried to hug Anna, but she wanted nothing to do with them. She was in shock.

"Should I have the man call an ambulance so you can go to the hospital and be checked?" Laura asked Anna.

Anna just sat there, arms around herself rocking in a chair.

Chapter 15

The policía finally arrived. One *oficial* questioned Laura and asked why she was in the country.

"Where are you staying?" he asked Laura in English.

"I'm staying with a host family, the Valverdes, out of Limón."

"What happened?"

"There were four of us on the north shore of Playa Soledad watching a turtle lay her eggs. Our friend Gabriel was taken. I remember seeing a masked man hit him with his gun, and before I could register what was going on, someone had come at me from behind. I tried to kick at his shin, and my elbow hit him."

"And you're sure this person was male?" asked the officer.

"I'm assuming based on the strength of lifting me. Anyway, I was punched in the stomach and my head was covered and my wrists bound. The man threw me into the back of what I think was Gabriel's vehicle. They pushed Gabriel into it also. One of the men was next to me. He held me down. I'm guessing that there were at least four of them. I remember driving over smooth roads, then bumpy roads with lots of potholes, and knew we were away from the beach because the road was paved," Laura said. The relief of seeing law enforcement and pent up tension made her rush her words.

"Where is your friend, Gabriel, now?"

"I'm not sure. I heard sounds. A scuffle. Gabriel was pleading with them. Vehicles drove away. They've taken him!"

"What time did all of this occur?"

"I don't know. We started at about 8:30 p.m. I guess we walked around the first section of beach for about 30 or 40 minutes looking for turtles nesting before we moved further north."

"Where were the others at this time?"

"We were all together. Gabriel had pointed out turtle tracks and we all got out of his truck to find them. We had phones with us and flashlights, but those were taken away when we were shoved into a shack."

"Did anyone else know you would be on that beach?"

"There are usually four security officers driving along the beach for extra eyes and ears. I remember that Gabriel had checked in with them when we started out and he told us that everything had been reported as normal and quiet."

"Had there been anything unusual before the shift or earlier in the week? Had anyone made threats to you before?" the officer asked.

Laura felt comforted by the questions. At least someone was watching out for them.

"Anna and I did see some damaged nests, and an area where a turtle had been beheaded. A week ago, when we saw that dead turtle, there were foot prints to and from the water. Earlier, Bianca and I thought we were followed around town by a blue and white motorcycle. But we weren't sure. When we were at the beach last week, a skinny guy jumped out at us with a machete and told us to stop the walks.

"I know that Gabriel had been trying to get more security patrols for the beach. Poaching and vandalism to turtle nests was happening almost every night. Daniela Segura is the Director of LSTC. She might be able to give you more information on that. She worked closely with Gabriel on the program for Playa Soledad." Laura was sure she was rambling.

"How can we reach her?"

"LSTC has a twenty-four-hour emergency number. I don't have it on me, I'm sure you can find the number. Someone can get a message to her. She tries to check in with each of us weekly to see how things are going and if we need anything. How much longer will this take? Can we go home soon?"

"We're almost done. I'll have someone call the Valverdes for you."

"You need to find Gabriel. We were in a shack and Bianca thought it might be one of those raft launching places. I'm really worried about him I'm afraid he might be hurt and needs medical attention. I'm sure they were beating him."

"I'll make a call and see if we can get additional *oficiales* to look into that."

Laura was exhausted, dirty, her throat dry, her feet raw, and her wrists aching from the rope burn. She wanted to sleep, but was wide awake.

***

The bright sun and the cacophony of early morning bird song had started as Clemente Valverde arrived to get Laura. She had never been so happy to see a friend and gave him a hug as the waterfall of tears started. The police told her and her friends to stay nearby for the next couple of days for more questioning.

In Clemente's car she put her head back, closed her eyes, and shut out the last several hours, the night kept replaying in her mind. Where is Gabriel? Is he ok? How long had the men been hiding along the beach? Could the security patrol been involved because no one came to help? Or, did they kidnap the patrol officers as well?

***

Back at the Valverdes, Laura reached for the phone. "I have to let Daniela know what happened. Maybe she can find where Gabriel is."

Daniela heard the story and said, "Laura, I hear the fear in your voice, I've contacted the Limón policía already. Bianca and Anna also called. I'm on my way, I'll be there in a couple of hours. Try to get some rest."

Laura went to clean up and add first aid cream to her wrists then went back to her room. She fell asleep from pure exhaustion and dreamt about Gabriel, remembering when they went to Punta Uva just a couple of days ago. After taking the necessary beginner Scuba lessons in shallow water, she had progressed and was ready to dive in deep waters. She used her spare time to take the local bus south to the dive shack in Puerto Viejo. The dive with Gabriel was her first and she had been nervous, the thought of swimming with sharks, stingrays and fish her size was a bit scary.

She'd been more comfortable watching the experienced divers from a distance. Gabriel reassured her, let her work at her pace. He pointed out where the green turtles hung out and encouraged her to come along. The turtles were so graceful in water. Above a green turtle, Laura thought it was about the size of her torso.

Gabriel had shown her much of the Caribbean coast, its culture and the wonder of marine life.

Her dream mind shifted. She was on a bus, that skinny guy she saw in the internet café and who had asked her to dance was also on the bus. Staring at her. Confusion. Was this real? Had he been on that bus? Why was this guy in her dream?

**

She'd been asleep for a couple of hours when Maria and Daniela woke her. "Laura, they found Gabriel," Daniela said.

Laura recognized that Daniela had been crying, her eyes red and swollen. "Is he ok? Where was he?" Laura asked sitting up.

Daniela said "I just spoke with the policía. A passerby saw a naked body on Playa Soledad this morning. It's been identified as Gabriel. He was found next to his vehicle, naked and beaten. The policía think he was dragged through the sand. They found him at the north shore of Playa Soledad. The medical examiner is looking at cause of death now. We should have results in a couple of days."

"NO!"

Daniela and Maria reached in to hug her. Laura was devastated. She'd only known him for the short time she had been in the LSTC volunteer program, they'd spent so much time together she'd considered him a brother. Tears ran as she stared into space. She left an ordinary world to come to an extraordinary one, new friends, new language. She'd found peace and relaxation. Costa Rica's landscape and wildlife was a kaleidoscope of beauty. With this news, it now seemed no better than the one she'd left.

Daniela realized that Laura would need some time alone, as she herself needed time. "I'll call the others. We'll need to meet tomorrow and decide what to do. I'm suspending patrols on Playa Soledad. It's not worth losing human life," Daniela said.

"You can't do that. The hueveros and drug smugglers win. What about all those eggs we've been able to save?" Laura wailed.

"I'll suggest our security be moved to focus on those already relocated so we can release them back to the sea when the time comes. I know a couple of people who can keep an eye on them. The conservation community and LSTC will have to work together to fight and push our government and MINAE for change. Word will get out about Gabriel, and the conservation community will support us. You get some rest and call your family back in the states. Let them know that you're alright and you'll be home soon."

***

Daniela was stoic giving Laura the news. Inside she was mess. She had known Gabriel for several years. She felt responsible and was angry at the lack of cooperation from the policía and MINAE. This never should have happened. She drove to the hatchery and sat on the beach staring at the water while thinking about the next steps. She was alone, her friend was gone, her tears came in floods. She would have to send the women home. Perhaps if she offered a reward someone might come forward. She knew that if drugs were involved the locals may fear for their lives and not speak up, but she had to try something.

Chapter 16

The next morning, the *Tico Times* and other local and national news networks featured stories about Gabriel and the alleged "narco-poaching" events at Playa Soledad. Daniela would need to move quickly to get the OIJ in on the investigation and get the women home before they became part of the media storm.

Wendigo caught a report on the radio. Furious, he immediately called Esteban. "What the hell were your guys doing? Have you seen the news? I said no one was to be hurt. This is catastrophic. This means we will need to lie low on the shipments for a while because everyone will be watching that coastline. Do you know how much money we will lose? And if your guys get caught, it will not be traced back to me. I have people in high places." Specifically, his friend Rafael Rodriguez Sanchez of MINAE.

"I understand. I was so busy with the shipment and making the deadline, I didn't survey the beach. I just learned about it this morning myself. Don't worry, I'll figure out a way to deal with the men, I always do." Esteban slammed the phone. He wanted blood.

***

Daniela met with the volunteers at the hatchery and announced she was suspending the program on Playa Soledad. "I want to let you know that your respective consulates have called and they urge you to go home immediately." Anna was quick to agree, she was ashamed and embarrassed by what happened. She didn't want to be a part of the investigation.

"I'm going to join my husband in New York. I'll leave in a couple of days. I've already spoken to him," Bianca said, "Nothing like your life being threatened to put things into perspective."

"I'm not leaving. They won't win. They've taken the peacefulness I was feeling and I'm fighting back. They've also taken a friend and I won't run away. I need to fight in memory of Gabriel," Laura stood tall, balled fists at her side.

"You're crazy, Laura. You should go home. Be safe. This isn't your battle," Bianca said.

"Gabriel was a wonderful, caring, patient human being. He didn't deserve to have his life ended so soon. I'm really pissed off about this and I want to find and bury that guy with the horrid breath that grabbed me. Let me go to San José with you." Laura took Daniela's hand, "I can help do research, I can be a witness and speak for Gabriel to MINAE. I can protest.

"You've got to let me help. I need to do this for Gabriel. I need to do this for myself. I don't want to leave this country under these circumstances. I want to fight back. I still have four weeks paid for and no one is expecting me. Let me be an advocate with you."

"Bianca's right, this isn't your battle. I tend to agree with the consulate, you should go home," said Daniela.

"What about you?" Laura pressed Daniela's hand harder, "You need support too. We can't forget that you also lost a friend. You knew him better than we did. You must be hurting. Let me help. We can help each other heal."

"I'll think about it. In the meantime, a liaison from the OIJ will be joining us soon. The investigation has been elevated from the regional level and he wants to take your statements again." Daniela doodled over her notes.

***

Mid-day they gathered at the Valverde residence to continue the business in a cooler and dryer location. "Ladies, this is the lead investigator from the OIJ, Antonio De La Torres," Daniela said. "I have worked with Antonio a couple of times in the past about security. He comes from the San José OIJ office and has agreed to help lead this investigation into Gabriel's death and your kidnappings. He'll also be working with the regional team here in Limón. He knows you've given information to the Limón policía, but is hoping you've remembered something new from the other night, and he might pick up something from your stories the Limón policía didn't."

Laura was impressed by Antonio's athletic build and he emitted a warm presence in the group meeting. She felt comfortable and nervous in his presence at the same time. Daniela started the process, the first to interview with Antonio. She had explained her relationship with Gabriel, how they met, and the length of time they'd been patrolling that beach. "Have you run into hueveros on your previous patrols?" asked Antonio.

"Yes, each turtle season. The locals gather as many eggs as they can to sell or trade, in some cases for drugs. Last year Gabriel and I were able to build a relationship with a couple of individual hueveros because we ran into them often. We were able to negotiate with them, educate them on why the leatherbacks were threatened, why the eggs are important, and save some of the eggs they'd taken. All recent reports from Gabriel indicated that the number of hueveros seems to have increased." Daniela said.

"Were you or Gabriel threatened last year, or had you seen any violence on the beach?"

"We both had been warned to stop the patrols, but were able to get the Limón policía to do several patrols in the area while we walked the beach. The additional security joined us on walks and were armed with AK-47s themselves. We had twice the amount of security last year than we did this year." Daniela looked down at her hands.

"Why did you continue the program this year?"

"We hoped we could have a better season, hoped that the laws would be enforced and that we would have better security this time." Daniela bit her lip, then continued. "We had the security lined up with the Limón policía until I received a letter from them just before the nesting season peaked in May. They said there were several reasons they would not be able to offer as much support this year. We were lucky we got the five we had. By that time, several of the volunteers had already arrived. That's why I started calling OIJ and spending more time in San José, trying to work with MINAE and MSP to do something about enforcement and protection."

"When did you first notice the increase in poaching traffic and vandalism this year?" Antonio asked.

"Just a couple of weeks ago. We started the program in February, everything was calm and quiet until the first of May. Our foreign volunteers were the first to report the increased activity in the early morning shifts." Daniela's desperate eyes met Antonio's. "They had not been threatened at that point, but they did tell Gabriel that they thought they were being followed. Reports that Gabriel sent me said there was competition and the poachers were aggressive. He speculated a new gang of hueveros was working the beach and one of them reportedly carried a machete. He had recorded evidence of a be-headed turtle and we suspected this group."

Antonio made notes before continuing. "What time did Gabriel and the volunteers start their shifts that night?"

"I don't know. The last shift was usually sometime between 9 and 10 p.m. and would go till about midnight or 1 a.m. The *oficiales* on patrol didn't want to stick around much after midnight so I encouraged Gabriel to stop when the patrols stopped."

"The hueveros that you negotiated with, do you think they are responsible?"

"No. I think they just wanted to earn the money from the eggs. I honestly don't think they would hurt anyone. This has got to be the new group. There was a new guy that Gabriel mentioned he would run into every once in a while. The guy had been laid off from the ports and his description seems to match the man Bianca and Laura described as the person they thought had been following them. I think Gabriel said the name was Juan Carlos Martinez."

"I did receive information the local policía had received other reports of armed men on the beach. Not sure who called in the information, but I'll look into that further," Antonio added as he jotted down the name.

***

Antonio spoke with Bianca next.

She began, "I overheard the men with us in the vehicle mention something about meeting a boat and shipments. Anna was with me, but I don't think she understood the Spanish. I know they had guns on us. At one point I felt that one of the men leaned toward Anna. She had been screaming and kicking and she suddenly stopped and got quiet. I heard a second man whispering something in Spanish but with the noise of the vehicle I couldn't understand. I think we were in a van. There was room for multiple people and the seats were on the side, but not like in an SUV. One more thing I remembered, Laura and I thought we'd both been followed a couple of days ago. I was at Mercado Central when I saw a young skinny guy, thought he might have a tattoo, something shaped like an S on his arm. I don't know if it's related, but I thought it worth mentioning."

Antonio thanked her for her time and made an additional note.

As Anna came in for her interview, she said, "One of the men whispered disgusting sexual threats to me. He touched my leg and put his hand up my shirt. I kept trying to make noise, and kick or hit him. Then, someone stuck the end of a gun in my stomach. I stopped moving after that. Before they pushed me into that shack, one of the men hit me and gave me a bloody nose. He pushed me to the floor and raped me. This whole experience has been degrading and disgusting and I really just want to go home." Anna started to cry again.

"I don't have a report from the Limón policía that you reported the rape. Had you seen a doctor, did you tell one of the others?"

"No, I just want it all to go away. I screamed and no one could help me. By the time the police arrived at that nice man's house, I had already washed my face. The policía didn't mentioned that I needed to see a doctor."

"That's too bad. We still have time to get a swab and test DNA. This will help us find your attacker. I understand that you just want to get home, but I can arrange for someone here to do that."

"I don't want anyone else to touch me!" Anna protested.

Laura repeated her story a third time when Antonio questioned her. "As I've been replaying the events of that night, a couple of things don't make sense to me. Why weren't our feet bound? Where was the security patrol officer assigned to that portion of the beach? And, if he was nearby, wouldn't he have heard our screams? I remember a deep voice threatening to shoot if we weren't quiet. He said no one was around to hear us. Did they also kidnap one of the officer's?"

"Interesting questions," Antonio notated more information, "I'll look into that."

He admired Laura's honey-gold hair tied back in a high ponytail as she had been twirling it in her fingers. He was enchanted by her blue grey eyes with what he thought were flecks of gold in them. At least that's what it looked like as the sun from the window hit her face. He thought of the stereotypical "California Girl" from magazines. Perhaps he would find more excuses to speak with her.

"When will you be leaving Costa Rica?" Antonio asked.

"I'm hoping Daniela will let me stay a few more weeks. I want to do what I can to help. I'm hoping she will let me go to San José with her. I want to help her with the MINAE meetings." Laura looked hopeful.

"Here's my card. Give me a call if you think of anything else we should know. It could be helpful to have you nearby while we continue to collect information," Antonio felt his face redden.

Chapter 17

A couple of days passed, and the medical examiner's report was filed. Gabriel's death was found to be asphyxiation from sand that had been forced down his throat. They also found evidence of blunt force trauma to the head.

Antonio researched a Juan Carlos Martinez from the Limón area and found he was dead. The basic information on him did seem to match Laura's description. He would dig deeper into his family background to see if it would turn up any additional leads and have the investigation team look into the women's cell phone numbers to check any recent activity.

***

"I still can't believe you talked me into this," Daniela said, driving west through the steady rain. "You're right, though, I can use the assistance and support. If MINAE hears your testimony, it could increase the urgency for security on the beaches. I want to encourage them to make Playa Soledad a national park with armed rangers year-round. It'll be good to have you as a sounding board for new ideas and have the extra manpower for research and letters." She paused, "By the way, you'll be staying in my condominium. I have to warn you it's small, just one bedroom and one bath, adequate kitchen for one person. Nothing fancy."

"I'm sure it will be fine. Thanks for letting me help. I'm curious to see how the Costa Rican government works." Laura kept her eyes on the two lane road. It felt like they'd descended into a tunnel of greenery.

"I have a laptop at home you can use. I hope you've learned Spanish well, because all government related websites and business are in Spanish."

"Good to know. I'm used to speaking about turtles, the beach, and basic everyday needs. I'll do some additional homework. I can read and understand it better than I can speak and write it. But, there is always Google translator." Laura started making a "task" list.

"I'll stay with my parents while you're at my place. You'll need the space. My mother can use the extra help and I can spend a little more time with my father. He helped start LSTC so he may have some ideas and contacts we can use."

"Are there any meetings scheduled with MINAE? And, I'm assuming we'll be traveling together?"

"Yes. There's one on Tuesday at 10 a.m. and the Minister of Public Security will also attend. We have a few days to prepare. However, the local Ticos have scheduled a candle light vigil for Gabriel at the MINAE building tonight. I'll be letting everyone know there will be a reward for information and arrest. We have a couple of hours to freshen up if you want to go." Daniela checked the rearview mirror.

"Of course. Is there a mall nearby? I only have one sundress and mostly shorts and tank tops, I'd like to find something a little more suitable to wear to the meetings."

"Avenida Central in San José is a pedestrian mall with boutiques and shops, or The Mall San Pedro. It's about 30 minutes away and one of the first malls in Costa Rica. It has boutiques and a cinema, many shops you might be familiar with from the Estados Unidos."

"Is there one you would suggest?" asked Laura.

"I think The Mall San Pedro will offer more options."

"Have you heard anything from Gabriel's parents regarding a service for him? I still can't believe he's gone." A tear formed in the corner of Laura's eye.

"Not yet, but I should hear soon. Probably within the week. I'm guessing they'll have it near their home in Cahuita." Daniela reached into her purse for a tissue.

"Will you go? And, can I come with you?"

"Yes, I'll be there, and I'll tell his parents that you would like to pay your respects also. I'll keep you posted."

"How well do you know Antonio De La Torres?"

73

"I met him last year as part of the meetings with MINAE, OIJ and MSP. Handsome isn't he?" Daniela glanced over to look at Laura.

"Mmmmm. Nice muscle definition. I found him to be just a little intimidating. Will he be attending the meetings?" Laura asked trying to keep her curiosity in check.

"I don't know. I'll be following up with him on the investigation, and I'm sure he'll be reaching out to clarify information."

"Do you trust him as an investigator? I know that you and Gabriel were frustrated with the police in Limón. They didn't appear to take much action."

"He seems authentic. What choice do we have? We have to trust someone. And, this is how the system works. We can only do our part." Daniel saw the tourist sign ahead.

"We are coming up on Braulio Carrillo National Park. We drove through it on our way to the Valverdes. There is a break in the rain and we're making good time. Do you want me to stop at any of the lookout points? Braulio Carrillo is a rainforest that happens to be between two volcanos, so it's very lush, or have you seen enough with the trips from LSTC?"

"No, that would be nice. I need to stretch my legs a little. Maybe take a couple of photos. How far are we from Heredia?

"We're about an hour away.

"Great. I'm eager to settle in."

Chapter 18

Manuel learned about Laura staying in Costa Rica and moving to San José through his channels at the policía and thought he better give Esteban a call. "I've just learned that the blonde woman from the Estados Unidos is going with that *Bruja* de *LSTC* to San José. The others are on their way out of the country. She thinks she can help with the investigation and plans on attending meetings with MINAE," said Manuel. "Also that investigator from OIJ wants to speak with the security detail. I've been able to avoid him so far. He is asking about who was assigned that stretch of beach and where they were that night."

"What did you tell your captain?" Esteban asked.

"That I'd seen a group of men with assault rifles wearing ski masks so I couldn't identify anyone. I was alone, I didn't have fire power to match and I knew that if I called it in, no one would come to assist. So I got the hell out of there. I knew that there were previous reports of a violent gang on the beach so I reminded him of that."

"Do you think he believes you?"

"Sí. He knows the department doesn't have the equipment to match assault rifles. The budget is so tight he doesn't have enough men to send out if he could. Besides, I have a good record and I've never given him any reason to doubt me."

"I hope that works. You're sure no one knows about your *other* job?"

"I'm confident it's still our secret."

"You better be. If anything changes, you know what can happen to you or your family." Esteban said as he poured himself a rum.

"I'm quite aware. I'll disappear for a couple of days so that OIJ oficial won't be able to interview me." Manuel heard the liquor gurgle.

"Wendigo was very angry about that death. Who was responsible?"

"The biologist was still unconscious when we pulled him out of the vehicle. Luis is the one that stripped him, tied him to the vehicle and drove around. Alonso and Pedro were gathering the eggs. Everyone was trying to keep themselves busy waiting for your return."

"And you just watched? You didn't stop it? You knew Wendigo said not to harm anyone." Esteban's face reddened.

"No. I don't know why. Luis was crazy. I was anxious to get the goods to shore and if he was in a drug craze, I didn't want to get involved. I wouldn't have been able to move the shipment."

"I'm gonna to teach that boy a lesson. Does your wife know about that night?"

"No, I haven't told her anything. Please don't hurt her."

***

Esteban updated Wendigo. "The investigation is heating up in the Limón area, especially with the security patrol. Manuel has been able to avoid being interviewed and is planning on disappearing for a while. I've warned him not to talk. I know who killed the biologist and I'll handle it. One more thing, the LSTC director and the woman from the U.S. are going to San José to meet with MINAE and OIJ. I'll have someone tail them and attend meetings as well."

"Sounds like things are under control. Keep tabs on the women. Do you have someone in mind?"

"Yes."

"Do you think this person can blend in?"

"Yes."

"Good. Stay informed and keep an eye on what Rafael is doing to delay responses. With the increased activity in Limón, we know that the Coast Guard and U.S. naval ships will be patrolling more often. I'll be moving the distribution point to the Pacific, and will use another liaison there. Your team has become a liability. I cannot afford more mistakes. This adds to our bottom line cost. I'm holding you responsible for that." Wendigo warned.

"Will we still need the processing facility in Pocora?" Esteban asked.

"I would suggest that you clean up and destroy anything that hasn't been shipped out. Everyone will need to lay low till the investigation is over."

"How do I pay the men?" Esteban asked

"They received a substantial amount in the last shipment, did they not?" Wendigo was becoming impatient.

"Yes."

"Then it's their problem. Don't you have some odd jobs they can do at the rafting business to keep them on the payroll at a reduced rate? I think it will be at least six months before any of this is forgotten." Wendigo hung up.

***

Deep canyons of green looked down onto a wide river of rapids as billowing clouds scudded through the grey skies. Daniela pulled up to the first lookout point overlooking Rio Patria. Laura got out of the vehicle and gazed at the emerald carpet that ran for miles up and down the hills. Taking a deep breath, she inhaled the scent of wet earth, dead leaves composting underfoot and the metallic smell of mud. "Another gorgeous view. What a beautiful country you live in." Laura appreciated the brief distraction.

"What is the name of that large leafed plant over there," asked Laura as she pointed.

"It's called the Poor Man's Umbrella," Daniela said.

"How appropriate. Looks like two people could hide under it. I've never seen such an enormous leaf."

At their second stop Daniela pointed and said, "We are now in Heredia Province, we call that volcanic mountain Cerro Cacho Negro. The Braulio Carrillo National Park, was named for one of our first Presidents. It became a national park when the road from Guapiles to the Caribbean was constructed because the locals were worried about deforestation. Scientists have found 6,000 different species of plants and 300 plus different types of birds."

"This must be impressive when the sun is shining. I don't have the vocabulary to adequately express what I'm viewing. You can also see the valley and the city beyond."

"Due to the elevation, it rains here a lot, even in the dry season. A sunny day is rare."

Chapter 19

At Daniela's, Laura walked into a room that was a combination of kitchen and living room, a large floor to ceiling window, and a small terrace. "Daniela, this is gorgeous and quite upscale from what I'm used to."

"Thank you. It's a couple of years old and I was able to get a great price for it. Let me show where to find the towels, and the other things you'll need." After a few minutes and a quick tour Daniela headed out. "Now, get yourself settled. I'll be back to pick you up for the vigil at about 7:30."

Laura, alone in a strange place for the first time in four weeks, felt the weight of the last week, and the death of Gabriel hit her in the silence. She was nervous, sad, and alone all at once.

***

Hundreds of people gathered with "Gabriel Viva" signs and black flags with the white outline of his face. The contrast was ghostly. Ticos carried large banners needing six people to hold them. Giant signs were hung from buildings on the Gonzalez Lahmann where the MINAE building was located. Laura couldn't believe the number of people gathered in the evening's drizzle to remember her friend. Children carried their plush turtles, locals and tourists held aloft handmade signs that read "save the turtles," "protect our beaches," and "justice now". They were chanting *"Gabriel viva, proteger nuestras playas"* meaning long live Gabriel, protect our beaches.

Daniela walked to the front of the group with a megaphone. "I'd like to thank everyone for their support this evening. Six other cities across Costa Rica are also honoring Gabriel." She continued with a short story about him and his commitment to conservation. "In his memory, I will be offering a $3,000 reward for the arrest and conviction of the person or persons involved in Gabriel's murder." There was applause. A marine biologist from the U.S, walked up to Daniela and asked her to use the megaphone. He announced that his global sea turtle organization would add an additional $10,000 to LSTC's reward. Louder applause.

Antonio De La Torres was also in the crowd. As he moved forward, he caught a glimpse of Laura in her bright yellow halter dress and smiled to himself as he moved toward her. "*Buenos noches*. I'm glad to see you were able to stay," he said as he moved toward Laura.

"*Buenos noches*. I didn't expect to see you here." Laura liked his smile and his neatly groomed two-day stubble and thought how attractive it looked on him.

"I received notification that a vigil was planned near MINAE. I thought I'd check it out. It's always nice to have *Oficiales de Paz* around in case violence breaks out."

"You don't really expect any violence do you?" Laura eyes widened.

"No, just my attempt at bad humor. I'm sorry, didn't mean to scare you."

"Oh. I'm still a little edgy. Have you found any suspects yet?"

"No, we had a lead on a Juan Carlos Martinez, but turns out he died prior to that evening. I'm waiting for results of geo-location on the cell phone numbers. We hope someone got careless."

"Did you ever find out what happened to the security patrol officer who should have been there that night?"

"That's not conclusive yet, still under investigation. My team has spoken with three of the five men and their alibi's check out."

"I see. Have you found anything else, any clues?"

"We have a couple of possibilities, not sure if they are related. Things don't move as fast here as you're probably accustomed to where you come from."

"Oh, I've never really had to think about it. I've just watched a lot of detective shows. Daniela and I plan to attend a meeting with MINAE on Tuesday afternoon, will you be there?"

Laura tried to keep a flirty tone out of her voice. This was business.

"Not something I'd scheduled, but I'll look into it. There could be useful information there. Thanks for the tip." Antonio kept up, trying to engage Laura in conversation while also wanting to appear serious about his investigation.

"Daniela wanted me to tell my story to the minister. I don't know what the protocol is, but if it helps to get better protection for the conservation community and expedite arrests, then I'll tell it again."

"What are your plans this weekend? I have a few other questions I'd like to ask."

"I'll be assisting Daniela with letters, a bill she wanted to introduce at the MINAE meeting, and I have an errand in San José I need to run that could take a good part of a day. Also, I hope to play tourist in San José. I'd really like to see the Teatro Nacional."

"Ah yes. The Opera House is one of the most beautiful buildings in San José. You've heard about the famous Italian ceiling mural?"

"Yes, I'm also a fan of Baroque style, so I'm eager to see the architecture and interior design."

"Perhaps I can meet you for a coffee somewhere when you're done? Where are you staying?" Antonio pressed a bit, wanting to see this woman again.

"I'll be staying at Daniela's place in Heredia, by the University. There is a coffee place down the street, I could meet you there. I'm not sure of the name though. Can I give you a call tomorrow and let you know what my schedule is looking like?"

Daniela's voice boomed from the megaphone again. She introduced a singer-guitar player who had written a song to honor Gabriel. The crowd hushed. Tears flowed, and the collective spirit of the crowd lent energy to the protests.

Chapter 20

Wendigo placed a call to the Minister of Environment Rafael Rodriguez Sanchez. "Rafael, I understand you'll be getting a visit from the LSTC Director regarding the death of her friend in Limón. She'll be bringing one of those volunteers with her. You are not to let that volunteer testify."

"We're getting pressure from many organizations because of that death. I can only delay what is inevitable so long. I serve at the pleasure of the *Presidente*, and when the pressure gets to that level, some kind of action will need to be taken." Rafael watched the latest update on TV as Wendigo's lecture droned on in his ear.

"Need I remind you, you're the Minister of Environment because of the contributions my family has made to the Presidente's advisors. You could be directing traffic in San José."

"I understand. You've been quite generous to our party. I'll delay decisions as long as possible. I suggest you use the same generosity with your connections in OIJ. Perhaps you can slow down their investigation. The conservationists have already had one vigil and I'm sure more protests will be held. We have postponed security as long as possible to this point," Rafael was impatient, "We'll need to take some short term action to placate people and convince the media that steps are being taken to improve and prevent future incidents such as this. In addition, we'll need money to delay the investigation on this end. You should know that OIJ has assigned one of their up and coming investigators to be the liaison on this case, one who is not easily influenced. You will want eyes in the regional offices to watch his moves."

"We have contacts in the Limón office. It won't be hard to buy more. Do you know the name of this liaison?" asked Wendigo.

"Antonio De la Torres. I'll keep you informed. Now, if that will be all, I have a meeting to get to." Rafael ended the call.

***

Antonio returned to his home near El Carmen in Guadalupe, just 15-minutes from where the vigil was held. He was pleased to see Laura Humphreys again and was determined to find a way to see her more often.

Antonio owed his mother a phone call. He checked in weekly. "Hola mama, I just wanted to be sure we are still on for church services Sunday? Are you up to going out for lunch after the service? My treat."

"Oh, mi hijo. Sí. You know I look forward to our Sundays. I have a few new friends I would like you to meet. I hoped you'd spend the day with me. I will make one of your favorite dishes. Just like when you were younger," she said. His father had passed away five years earlier, and he was relieved she had become so involved in her community and church.

"*Es un trato,* see you then." Antonio ended the call.

Sitting alone in his living room, a dull yellow light shown through from the kitchen. He put his feet up on his rustic wood table, and stared at the reddish brown vertical fissures and swirls in the finish. Drinking an Imperial, and thinking about the investigation, thoughts of Laura interrupted. He kept seeing her soft face, and knew she was a gentle spirit. He felt a twinge of arousal when he was near her, was drawn to her.

***

Following the vigil, Laura sat on the condo's stiff white sofa trying to find an English-speaking channel on television while checking her emails on her tablet. She logged into Facebook to see what her friends were up to. It had been several weeks since she'd cared about what was going on at home. Her time alone was valuable, but it had been an emotional couple of days. Her thoughts returned to Antonio. Daniela was right. He was quite handsome in a very rugged kind of way. Something had stirred in her that she hadn't felt in a long while and she hoped she would see him again soon.

***

Down the street a midnight blue Toyota Corolla had a view facing Laura's living room window. Alonso saw her draw the blinds as he finished his call to Esteban. He had followed Daniela and Laura home from the vigil and would be keeping an eye on her.

***

Morning sun reflected off the white walls and white coverlet waking Laura. As she lay in bed, she stared at her surroundings. Quiet. Alone. Space. The clock on the bedside table read 7 a.m., the longest she'd slept in since leaving the States. Where she'd felt protected and invincible earlier, she now felt vulnerable. The last several weeks replayed in her mind, she asked herself *Was I naive? I wanted space, a new start, to feel helpful. Was it necessary to leave home to accomplish that? Helping the turtles should have been harmless, why did it go so wrong? I know I was thorough in my research of the program and country.* The air conditioning unit above the bed, along with her thoughts, chilled her. *Get up and get moving, get off your pity pot and start fighting back.*

***

Following a cool shower, Laura found the traditional *Chorreador De Café,* the cloth filter, a tea kettle and the ground coffee. Adding a tablespoon of coffee to the filter for each cup, she poured in the boiling water. Finding bread, she cut a slice to toast. The blinds were opened, and she decided to enjoy her breakfast on the terrace.

Getting her bearings, the noise of traffic nearby, smell of exhaust, Laura watched pedestrians on their way to the university. The sun was out but clouds were gathering; it would be another rainy afternoon. The temperature was at least ten degrees cooler than in Limón.

Retrieving the laptop, she researched government agencies and reviewed the local news. Laura found an online English news forum with headlines describing the nose dive that tourism in the Caribbean had experienced after the reports of Gabriel's death. Still no arrests and it didn't appear there were any suspects, however, the investigation hadn't gone a full week yet.

After twenty minutes of searching the internet and only being able to translate a portion of the OIJ and MINAE websites, Laura grew frustrated and gave up. The realization of how much more Spanish would need to be learned to fit in to San José, hit her. A weekend of study would be needed to improve those skills. With no plans to meet Daniela today, Laura decided it would be a good time to check out the Teatro Nacional and hit the mall.

Having researched the directions to the opera house, the mall, and finding the nearest place to catch a cab, she turned off the laptop. Laura liked to know where she was going, and wasn't going to be conned by a cab driver. She would walk a couple of blocks to the University and catch a red cab there. It would take twenty minutes to get to the theatre, and the mall was only five minutes from there.

***

The blue Corolla had not moved. Alonso awoke with the sun and focused on the condo. He watched Laura move to the terrace, noted her long wet hair, light blue cotton knit robe, coffee mug. Wondered what she had planned for the day.

***

She grabbed an umbrella and was out the door. As she walked toward the university she heard a few cat-calls as she passed. *A woman alone in a Latin country, what were you thinking?* She forgot that Ticos were flirts. She picked up her step, didn't acknowledge the comments and whistles around her and grabbed the first available cab. An edge of intimidation took hold and she drew a deep breath to compose herself. She gave the cab driver the address and paid attention to his driving. Merging onto the Pan American Highway, traffic picked up.

***

Catching sight of her walking toward the university, Alonso started the engine and began to follow her. He stayed a couple of vehicles behind the cab and parked across from the theatre. She wore a bright yellow sun dress and was easy to spot.

85

Chapter 21

Laura's cab pulled up to the Teatro Nacional and she saw other cabs in the vicinity so didn't worry about catching another one. Paying her fare, she moved forward. The building was the most beautiful building she had seen in Costa Rica. The sandstone exterior and Italianate arched windows reminded her of the theatres in Western Europe and seemed out of place in this setting. The building was surrounded by an ornate wrought iron fence and gate. She paid her admission and signed up for the guided tour.

Walking past the Italian marble, statues, and gold leaf trimmed walls, she found the frescoed ceiling she'd read about, the balconies were as ornate as she'd seen in Europe. The tour took 30 minutes. Snapping a couple of photos with her tablet, she moved past a couple of people in her group and thought she picked up on a rotting scent. A flashback to that night on the beach hit her. She felt dizzy and grabbed the wall to steady herself, quickly left the theatre, and hailed a cab to the Mall San Pedro.

The mall was taller and longer than any mall in the U.S. When the cab driver dropped her off at the main entrance, several men crowded her offering their help or begging for money. She hastily made her way inside where the environment was more familiar.

The marble floors, airiness, and kiosks throughout the main floor were very similar to malls she was comfortable with back home. She found the directory and realized that there were over 200 stores and a large food court, and reminded herself of the task at hand.

Several hours of shopping passed, and Laura decided to take her four bags and go. Wanting to avoid the chaos at the entrance, she looked for another exit. A man about her height and weight had come around the corner. He saw she had several bags and said in Spanish, "Let me get the door, and call a cab for you."

"Gracias," she responded relieved for the help as she smiled at him. Moving past him, she smelled that horrible odor again. Stepping into the cab, another flashback hit and the hair on the back of her neck stood up. Her heart pounded, and she focused her breathing to bring the heartrate back down. She wanted to break into tears, but wasn't about to do that in a cab. Alonso watched as the cab drove off.

***

That afternoon, back in control of her nerves, she tried to reach Antonio. They agreed to meet at a Caribbean restaurant just a couple of blocks over from the condo at 5 p.m. That would give her time to put her new purchases away, freshen up and try out the new liner and lip tint before their meeting.

Daniela had phoned to say she'd pick Laura up Tuesday around 9 a.m. and that Gabriel's parents would have the service Wednesday near Cahuita.

***

Laura arrived a little early, grabbed a table near a window and ordered a mango *refresco*. Was it good form to meet an investigator at a restaurant? It was dinner time and she wanted to be in a public place. She also hoped he'd be less intimidating in a more casual environment. She watched the street for Antonio who was prompt. He walked towards the door in his faded blue jeans, torn at the knees, paired with a charcoal grey t-shirt. He didn't have an ounce of fat on him, he was all muscle. Checking her posture, she took another deep breath.

Antonio approached the door and spotted Laura in a soft pink sundress as she sipped a drink near the window. Her honey blonde hair was down and cascaded over her shoulders. He liked the more mature alluring look it gave her. He also detected a bit of cleavage from the deep V-neck of her dress that was attractive.

"Hello Ms. Humphreys" Antonio said. Laura thought his eyes seemed to be even darker and smokier than she remembered.

"Please, call me Laura." She extended her hand.

"Laura" he repeated. She loved the tenor of his voice; soft yet deep, and in combination with his Spanish cadence pronouncing English, *quite seductive* she thought.

"How can I help you?" she asked.

"I have a few questions and wanted to review my notes on a couple of things," he said.

"Sure, ask away."

"Shall we order something to eat first?" he asked.

"That would be nice."

They placed their orders with the waitress.

"How was your day? Did you get a chance to visit the Teatro Nacional?" he asked.

"Yes, it's beautiful. It reminded me of Europe, and honestly seemed to be a little out of place in San José," Laura relaxed, relieved to start the conversation with a little small talk. "I always enjoy murals, and had fun shopping. I'm surprised the mall is so similar to the one's back home." Their dinner arrived, and he moved on to more substantive questioning.

"The night of the kidnapping, you said nothing seemed unusual. Did you see the policía that was assigned to the area of the beach where you were?"

"No. I remember Gabriel calling them to check on the area and let them know we were out. Honestly, the security patrol usually just stayed in their cars, didn't interact too much with us. So I don't even have names to give you."

"Were the same men assigned to the same portion of beach each night?

"I think so."

"Would you be able to describe them?"

"I mostly worked the early shift and was assigned to the middle quadrant. I remember seeing the security car, and the blue uniform. The officer I saw had a thick hair, full face, maybe mid-40s. I was so busy learning the job and trying to make friends with the volunteers I didn't go out of my way to introduce myself. Looking back, that seems pretty rude." Laura picked at her salad.

"The night of the kidnapping, you never saw a security patrol officer when you went to the north portion of Playa Limón?"

"No. As I said, Gabriel made the phone call. We were focused on finding turtles and honestly hadn't paid attention to anything else around us."

"Do you remember hearing anything?" Antonio sliced a piece of plantain.

"Not until it was too late. I saw a figure out of the corner of my eye, Gabriel was hit in the stomach with the butt of a gun, and then arms were around me. Everything happened so fast."

"Do you remember Gabriel using the names of any of the policía?"

"No. I think he made a general call to whoever was in charge. Have you been able to speak to them, the security officers?" Laura asked.

"Not all of them. One seems to be conveniently unavailable, making me suspicious. The captain says this guy has been out ill for the last couple of days and he has not provided us this person's address. My supervisor needs to persuade the captain to give us this information."

"I see." Laura sipped her refresco.

"Had you been to the northern part of the beach previously?"

"Just a couple of times, I was mentoring Anna then. That was just last week. It seems so long ago now. Anna found the decapitated turtle. We saw footprints and fragments of a fire. There were also footprints to and from the water, but I told the police and you this earlier."

"Did you ever see any boats? Hear any noise in the vicinity at that time?" Antonio glanced at his notes.

"No. I thought the footprints were strange. I had the impression that someone had gotten out of a boat or a paddleboard or something that could get close to shore. I just didn't understand why they would be there in the early morning. I never saw a boat, never heard any voices, didn't smell any gas. It was dark on that shift. I could hear the surf, some birds, the monkeys, but I didn't hear voices beyond the people I worked with."

"How well did you know Gabriel? Had you met him previous to this trip?" Antonio took a bite of his fish.

"I only knew Gabriel for the four weeks I worked with the program. He was always courteous, but definitely serious about his mission. I remember Bianca and I would tease him often. Try to get him to laugh more. We realized that he seemed to relax most when we went on social events, so we would goad him into going out with us. Did you know he knew Latin dancing? He went out with us one night and taught us the Merengue. We had a lot of fun, lots of laughter. We were becoming good friends. I enjoyed our conversations, they were so easy." Laura smiled as she recounted those days before tragedy struck.

"We spoke about his childhood, why he loved his country and conservation so much. We talked about why I was here. I asked him to come visit me back in Northern California, as I know a couple of conservation groups there and thought I could introduce him. He took me scuba diving once and helped me to schedule the lessons. That had been something I always wanted to do, and because of him I did it." Laura dabbed away a tear.

"Did you have a romantic involvement with him?" Antonio asked tentatively.

The waitress stopped by to check on their needs, Antonio ordered a cerveza Imperial.

"No, he was more like a brother to me. I felt protective, grateful to have met him. I think he helped me be a better person. I know I've learned a lot from my time with him. I had recently ended a bad marriage. A relationship was the last thing on my mind."

"Why did you come here?"

"I wanted space… to find myself again. I felt like everything back home was an obligation. I stopped having fun. I wanted to come back to Costa Rica, and I was interested in marine conservation, so why not combine a sabbatical with eco-tourism?"

"Why didn't you go home when all the other volunteers did?" Antonio scribbled more notes.

"I don't know. I was angry, I didn't want fear to control me, and I want to help find Gabriel's killers. I don't want to see a good, well-meaning conservation program come to an end because of some outside corrupt activity. I don't want the drugs, or the poaching, or whatever it is that caused Gabriel's death to win. I want to fight. At Mall San Pedro today, the reality of my decision to stay and the cultural differences started becoming more obvious to me."

"What do you mean?"

"The cat-calls I got as I was walking to catch a cab. The group of men at the entrance to the mall almost rushing me when I got out of the cab. I realized that I don't really live here. I'm in a foreign country. I'm single woman alone, and men here seem to definitely recognize a woman alone. I think I'd just blocked that part out. I wanted to start life over in a new place, and I didn't think it through completely. Today I woke up alone for the first time in four weeks. The brain starts to get noisy when you're alone in a quiet environment." Laura looked at her hands and played with a ring.

"I'd have to agree with you there," Antonio said.

"What about you, are you married? Why did you decide to go into the OIJ?"

"No, never married. This job keeps me pretty busy. I lost a brother 10 years ago, drugs were involved. The perpetrators were arrested but received very light sentences. I wanted justice, so I thought I'd become part of that process. I attended the National Police Academy for a year following completion of the Criminal Justice program at the Universidad San Juan de la Cruz. Then I was selected to participate in the Fighting Drug trafficking training program that Colombia offered back in 2010. I know my superior assigned me this case because of that background." Antonio took a sip of his cerveza, "I work hard to be a good officer, I'm sure you've heard that many of the policía in this country take bribes. Well not this one. I want to find the truth and push for stricter sentences. I'm not the most popular guy in the group."

"I understand. Then it's good to know we're working with an honest cop. Are you going to the MINAE meeting Tuesday?" Laura smiled at him.

"Sí, I was able to work it into my schedule. I'm open to a new point of view and hope to get inspiration on other possible leads. Only time will tell."

"I look forward to seeing you there. Are there any other questions I can answer for you?" Laura blushed.

"Yes, just a few more. What do you know about the Valverdes, Clemente and Maria?"

"Why do you want to know? They aren't suspects are they?"

91

"I need to review all the host families and their backgrounds as part of the investigative process."

"I see. Well, I don't really know much about them to be honest. I trusted that LSTC did the background checks on them. Daniela told me she worked with them for several years. They've been easy to live with. They feel like an extension of family to me. I was relieved that Clemente came to get me the night of the kidnapping. I know that Maria stays at home, sometimes will help out as a volunteer, and they have two kids she looks after. I think Clemente is a manager near the docks somewhere. We never really talked about it."

"How long will you be in town?"

"I have about three weeks left on my sabbatical, but I could stay up to another four weeks on my passport. I'm not sure yet. We have the meeting Tuesday. Gabriel's service will be near Cahuita on Wednesday. It all depends on what has been accomplished by the end of the week. I sure would like to know that you've arrested someone before I leave, that would make my extended stay here worth it. Any headway today?"

"I'm afraid nothing new. I'll do my best to make an arrest as soon as possible. I expect to hear about the cell phone traces soon."

They finished their dinner and Antonio motioned for the check.

"It's dark outside, would you mind walking me home? I'd feel safer."

"My truck is right outside, how about I drive you back?"

Chapter 22

Antonio helped Laura into the passenger seat. She was nervous sitting side by side with this very attractive man. Minutes later, they walked to her door. There was a warm spicy scent about him and that caused her temperature to rise. "Thank you," she said inserting the key into the lock. "Can I offer you a glass of water while you're here, or maybe a cup of coffee?"

"Water would be fine. Thanks."

She invited him to sit on the sofa, and walked to the kitchen.

Antonio surveilled the room evaluating security. He couldn't help it, he was a cop. Not bad. Second floor and deadbolts, he thought. He returned his attention to Laura as she handed him the glass of water. *AWKWARD. what were you thinking? Do you sit by him or just keep standing? Do you make a move or just keep this professional?* she thought as she remained standing.

"Thank you. Do you usually keep your patio door locked?" he asked.

"Yes, the Valverdes told me that petty theft is quite common here. I try to keep things locked all the time. It's nice to sit out on the terrace in the morning though. That's ok, right?"

"Sure, just keep it locked when you come back inside. The second floor offers a little more protection. I also suggest that the next time you go shopping you take a friend."

"You're right, I'll call Daniela. I was overconfident and too independent today." They stared at each other with awkward smiles, neither one knowing what to do next.

Antonio spoke first, "Thank you for the water, I should be going. I'll see you at the meeting Tuesday. Let Ms. Segura know I'll have questions for her as well."

"Goodnight. Thanks for dinner, that was nice." she said softly as she walked him to the door. They shook hands and he turned to leave.

***

Alonso was in the same spot he was the previous night and spied the OIJ investigator walking the blonde back to the condo. He called Esteban with the evening report.

***

Still early evening, Laura had time for more research. She opened her laptop and queried, the Ministry of the Environment and Señor Rafael Rodriguez Sanchez. THE WEBSITE READ: *RAFAEL RODRIGUEZ SANCHEZ ATTENDED UNIVERSIDAD NACIONAL DE COSTA RICA EARNING A BACHELOR'S DEGREE IN ENVIRONMENTAL SCIENCE. HE ALSO ATTENDED YALE UNIVERSITY GRADUATING WITH A MASTER'S DEGREE IN ENVIRONMENTAL MANAGEMENT.*

SCROLLING DOWN THE PAGE: *HIS FUNCTION IS TO COORDINATE THE ISSUES REGARDING CONSERVATION AND NATIONAL RESOURCES.*

Pretty impressive Laura said to herself eager to learn more about how the government agency worked, knowing she'd have more questions for Daniela.

Laura continued her search on the OIJ. She learned the largest group of law enforcement was the *Fuerza Publica* (national police) operated by the MSP and they wore the blue uniforms similar to the security at Playa Soledad. They were the ones who'd questioned her in Limón after the kidnapping. A couple more links and she learned that OIJ did the investigations and undercover work. Reading local news articles on line, she concluded that the law enforcement system was inconsistent at best. Foreigners were more likely to be jailed if they committed crimes but not Ticos. It all depended on where the crime and location had been committed, but in her opinion law enforcement in the states was stronger.

She understood why Daniela pushed for meetings with the Ministries and OIJ, the consistent pressure from the people was what moved the process forward.

***

The slim black skirt she purchased hugged her hips enhancing her figure. The hound's-tooth print blouse billowed, softly tucked in above the waist. Her honey blonde hair draped over the collar and onto her shoulders. She applied the basic shadow, eye liner and lip stain and began to look like her old corporate self. She liked what was reflected in the mirror. Her skin had tanned golden and the liner set off the blue grey of her eyes. It had been a nice break living in shorts, tank tops and swimsuits, no fuss. Time to get down to business. She hoped Antonio would find the change attractive too. Laura would bring out the confident, intelligent, assertive side she'd tucked away.

***

Daniela and Laura climbed the front steps of MINAE and took the side stairway leading to a second-floor conference room furnished with black and chrome furniture. Three long black Formica topped tables with chrome legs were at the front of the room with several chairs arranged in rows assembly style. The walls were plain white with a projection screen centered on the front wall and the Costa Rican flag hung from a stand next to it. Laura followed Daniela to their seat at the table on the right. Laura assumed that the Minister of Environment would be sitting at the table front and center. People started to fill in the seats behind them and she asked Daniela, "Who will be sitting at the other table?"

"A business contingent from Limón," Daniela replied. "They've been experiencing cancellations due to Gabriel's death and related media stories."

"I read something about that the other night online." Laura said.

Rafael entered through a side door. He was wearing a deep chocolate brown tailored suit with a cream button-down shirt and a shiny satin cream tie, his dark hair slicked back, he was short and stocky, about five feet six inches, and she thought he was trying too hard to be "Euro Chic." He sat down at the center table as expected. A second man joined him.

Laura whispered to Daniela. "Who's the other man?"

"The Minster of Public Security," Daniela whispered back.

95

Laura scanned the room, caught a glimpse of Antonio a couple rows back across the aisle and smiled. At the rear of the room, hidden from sight, Alonso sunk into a chair. Rafael called the meeting to order and acknowledged Daniela, the other conservation organizations in attendance, and the group of Limón business owners. He said a few words in condolence of Gabriel Montenegro and then called on Daniela.

"We are here today to ask the government for assistance. Our beaches need more security and protection. Our employees and volunteers should be able to work in a safe environment, and I know the result of my friend's death has had an effect on the tourist industry and businesses in Limón Province. My organization and others in the conservation community have offered a reward for the arrest and conviction of those responsible for Gabriel's murder. I have also drafted a proposal requesting that Playa Soledad become a national park to include park rangers with the power to make arrests and named in honor of Gabriel Montenegro.

"I have a guest with me today as well. Someone who was there the night that Gabriel was murdered and she has agreed to answer any questions you may have." The room broke out in applause as she concluded her speech.

The business owners also spoke, agreeing with Daniela. They let the ministers know they'd had a 50 percent cancellation rate in the last week because foreigners were afraid to travel to Limón Provence. They also advocated for the National Police having stiffer penalties and actual enforcement to discourage drug use, poaching, theft, and violent crimes in the area.

The ministers kept order, and everyone had a chance to speak except Laura. Rafael closed the meeting two hours later, "We thank you for the information you've shared today. We'll take your recommendations and comments under consideration. Regarding Playa Soledad as a national park, we will need to conduct feasibility studies." There were a few groans in the room but Rafael continued, "There is pending development in the area, both residential and commercial, and we'll need to consider that impact on this proposal. Another possibility would be to create a memorial fund to be used in some manner to recognize Mr. Montenegro and his conservation efforts. The MSP and I plan on touring Limón very soon so we can hear from the residents. This meeting is adjourned."

"He never called on me," Laura leaned toward Daniela.

"We'll need to find out when they'll be in Limón and try again. I think they're just delaying decisions. The depth of this meeting seemed to be too shallow and conciliatory." Daniela shrugged. Laura understood most of the meeting conducted in Spanish, but was overwhelmed with the amount of the language she'd need to grasp.

Chapter 23

Antonio ran to catch-up with Daniela and Laura as they were leaving the conference room. "Good afternoon ladies. Ms. Segura, do you have a few moments? I would like to ask you a few questions."

"Right now? Here?" Daniela asked.

"Yes," Antonio said.

"Is there some place more private?"

"Let's walk outside."

The three continued down the stairs and outside. Antonio motioned to a quiet corner.

"You mentioned there were a couple of hueveros you and Gabriel had negotiated with last year. Do you remember their names?" Antonio leaned against a wall.

"Why do you ask?" Daniela cast a puzzled expression at him.

"The policía in Limón arrested two hueveros early this morning. These men claim they know nothing about the death. Their names are Orlando Araya Lopez and Francisco Morales Guillermo. Are those names familiar to you?"

"Sí. They're the two we spoke with. Are they suspects?"

"Not at the moment, they're being held for poaching. I'm heading to Limón when we're done here to go question them myself. You mentioned earlier you didn't think they were capable of harm. Do you still feel that way?"

"Yes. Poverty is an issue in Limón Province. Orlando and Francisco are just making a living the best way they can. Gabriel mentioned that Orlando warned him not to walk the beach alone. Maybe they have information that could help find who did this." Daniela absently glanced at people walking by.

"That's what I'm hoping for. Did you know Gabriel offered to pay Orlando for eggs?"

"We did that a year ago, before I started running the Conservancy. I'm not aware that Gabriel had done that since."

"You and Laura, um, Ms. Humphreys are going to Cahuita tomorrow for the services, correct?"

"Sí. I'd like to get an early start. The plan is to stop at the hatchery first to check with security on the progress of eggs, as a couple of groups are due to be released soon. I've been told they've increased security patrols since Gabriel's death. Seems senseless to add staff now and not when we requested it." Daniela shook her head in dismay. "You've heard that I suspended the program on that beach. Right? I want to see for myself what exactly the new security is. You have my cell number. I'll have it off during the service, but if you need more information, I'm more than happy to return your call."

Antonio peered down at this notes. "Clemente and Maria Valverde, how long have they been a host family?"

"We've worked with them for the last five years, why?"

"When I was questioning Ms. Humphreys, she mentioned that he was a manager somewhere near the ports, is that right?"

"Sí. He manages one of the banana export companies. His team does the maintenance on the ships. His wife, Maria, has also been a volunteer for us. What does this have to do with the investigation?"

"Just need to get a sense of the host families. Was Señior Valverde involved in any of the recent layoffs?"

"I don't know. You'd have to ask him."

"Ms. Humphreys mentioned you perform background checks on the host families. Do you do checks every year?"

"No, we run the background check when a family expresses interest in being a part of our organization. We wouldn't re-run one unless something unusual occurred. That has never happened, though." Daniela crossed her arms in front of her.

"I appreciate your cooperation. By the way, we've had a lead on a couple of the cell phone numbers from the phones taken. I'm hoping to interview a couple of those people as well."

"Thank you. I appreciate your efforts with the investigation and in keeping me informed." Daniela extended her hand.

"I'll be going. It's a long drive to Limón," Antonio said as he nodded farewell, shook her hand and walked away.

Laura had been standing off to the side. She came up with an idea waiting for the conversation to end. "Daniela, what if I emailed my Congressmen and contacted the media where I live and let them know what happened? Maybe my government can pressure Costa Rica." Laura said.

"It can't hurt. I know the global conservation community has more rallies planned. We'll need to act fast to keep the pressure on MINAE and the policía. Can you do that tonight before we leave in the morning?"

"Yes, I'll get right on it. There are a couple of conservation programs where I live. I'll contact the television stations there and see if I can get them to do a story. I'll ask our citizens to also write their congressmen. We could build momentum for action."

A man brushed by Laura quickly. His head was down, she sensed something familiar but she didn't know why.

"That's sounds great. Is there anything you need to pick up before we head back to the condo?" Daniela asked. "Laura, are you ok?"

Laura was still; her face ashen.

"Did you notice that person that just passed me?" Laura asked.

"No. why?"

"It's the second time in two days that I've had a weird feeling. I had a flashback to that night on the beach."

"I'm afraid I didn't see him or notice anything unusual. I'm sorry." Daniela's expression became concerned.

"I must be light headed. Would you mind if we stopped for a quick bite to eat? I haven't eaten since this morning." Laura's hand touched her forehead as she tried to gain composure. "You don't mind do you?"

"No. Not at all, what kind of food did you have in mind? Vegetarian, Brazilian, Italian, Japanese? You can find them all in San José."

"Do you know a good burger joint? I haven't had one since I've been in Costa Rica. I've been trying all the traditional foods." Laura hoped some comfort food would make things better.

"There is a little bar and grill in one of the hotels that's been voted "Best Hamburger in Costa Rica" how about that?" Daniela said.

"Sounds perfect. Thank you."

***

Alonso had shadowed the group out the door and quickly moved past Laura, brushing her arm. He heard something about cell phones and "lead" but had moved to quickly to grasp the entire conversation. He called Esteban to let him know that Rafael did not question Laura and kept the meeting brief. Esteban was pleased to hear this and immediately informed Wendigo.

Chapter 24

Antonio pulled into the Limón Police Station late in the afternoon. He'd just missed the chief but could speak to the two hueveros, deciding he'd spend the night and catch the police chief in the morning. Antonio worked his way through the building to the holding cells. The scent of old plaster and peeling metal along with the rancid stench of urine mixed with days old sweat became stronger as he came closer to the group of men behind bars. Antonio never got used to that smell.

"Which one of you is Orlando Araya Lopez?" Antonio eyed the ten men crammed together in the small cell. Orlando and Francisco, two young men in shabby clothes, had huddled together on one of the three benches afraid to move. The other men in their cell were older, larger and covered in tattoos.

"I am," Orlando stood up and walked forward hoping he would be getting out of there.

"You were arrested for poaching sea turtle eggs early this morning on Playa Soledad. Where on the beach did this occur?" Antonio asked.

"The central part of the beach, why do you need to know?"

"You're an acquaintance of Gabriel Montenegro and Daniela Segura. correct?"

"I met them a year ago. They paid me for the eggs they caught me holding."

"I see, and this year?"

"I only saw Gabriel once in a while. I haven't seen Daniela at all."

"Did Gabriel buy eggs you'd taken this year?" Antonio looked at his notepad.

"No, we had come to a first come first served agreement."

"That sounds like a pretty good deal for you, more money in your pocket, correct?"

"That's what I hoped," Orlando studied the cockroach that was crawling over his sneaker.

"Success wasn't so good this year?" Antonio looked at him under furrowed eyebrows.

"Not really. There was more competition on the beach."

"Is that so, what kind of competition? Do you typically work the entire beach?"

"Last year me and Francisco and a handful of other people were the only ones on this beach." Orlando looked over at Francisco for support. "This year a new gang moved in. I'd heard rumors that one huevero carried a machete, and others on the beach had been threatened. These rumors came from the north part of the beach, where there are more trees, so we avoided that area and stayed on the lower parts."

"I see. What do you do with the eggs once you have them?" Antonio continued making notes.

"Sell them."

"To who?"

"There are a couple of local vendors," Orlando made eye contact.

"How much do you make when you sell them?"

"On a good night we can make up to 500,000 *colones*."

Antonio whistled, "That's about $1,000, that's a lot of money. So, what makes a 'good night'?"

"Depends on the month. Usually May, June and September are best."

"How many turtle nests would that be that you've looted in one evening?"

"Could be 10"

"Why do you do this?"

"It is my business" Orlando said.

"How did you get into that business?"

"I don't have any other job, I didn't finish school, and I need to eat. Francisco showed me how to make money." Orlando pointed out Francisco to Antonio

"Where do you live?"

"In a shack a few miles from the beach."

Antonio couldn't really blame these two pathetic looking men for just trying to survive, but continued his questioning. "When was the last time you spoke to Gabriel Montenegro?"

"A few days before he was found dead."

"What was the occasion?" Antonio asked.

"Gabriel was walking the beach. I was on the northern part that night with Francisco and several other friends. We had a bonfire and were drinking rum. Gabriel stopped to say hello and I offered him a drink."

"You weren't afraid to be on the northern shore that night?"

"I was with several friends." Orlando said.

"Were you doing drugs with these friends?"

Orlando got defensive "No way. Nasty stuff, I see what it does to people."

"Gabriel made a police report. It stated someone attending a party on the beach, saw another person with a machete. Are you the one that saw the machete?" Antonio looked him in the eye.

Orlando got quiet and looked away.

"It was you, wasn't it, Orlando. Why don't you want to tell me?" Antonio asked.

"These people are violent. They threaten to hurt others. I don't want to be hurt."

"Don't you want to help your friend Gabriel?"

"I can't help Gabriel. He's dead."

"Don't you want to help find his killer? Get them off that beach so you can go back to business?"

"I didn't see anything," Orlando raised his voice. "Not faces anyway. I was drunk. I passed out. When I woke up, I saw two guys, one had the machete. They were talking. I hid, I didn't want to die."

"But you saw two men. That's helpful, Orlando. Now we know two men may have killed your friend." Antonio made note and his tone became more encouraging.

Orlando's confidence increased, "I saw a third man join them."

"So, now we have three men, anyone else join them?"

"No, just the three."

"Did you notice their age, height, weight? Did they have long or short hair?"

"I think the first two guys were younger, maybe my age. The third guy seemed to be older, in charge of them. He called them '*idiotas.*' One of the guys might be about my size. The older guy was taller, wider, bald on top."

"What do you mean by wider? Was he fat? Did he look like a wrestler, for example?"

"Not fat, but bigger, more muscle than the other two. Bulky."

"Ok, Orlando. Now we're getting somewhere. We know we have three guys, two young, one older, one skinny, one bulky and bald. One had a machete. Did you ever see anyone bring drugs on the beach? Any boats nearby?"

"No, but I've seen people on the beach who I know were on drugs. I've also seen people sell drugs there. I don't know who they are, but I see things I don't want to see. I just try to stay on the beach in the early morning and get my eggs and sell them."

"Did you ever see the security patrol on the beach? Did they ever catch you before?"

"No. It's known that the security patrol leaves after midnight. We wait until they're gone to do our work. This is the first time anyone caught me. The policía have added more *hombres* now."

"Thank you Orlando, you have been helpful." Antonio then looked at Francisco and motioned him to come over. "Francisco, what about you? Where were you the night of the party?"

"I was there. Orlando was really drunk so he left earlier than me," Francisco said.

"What time did the party start, and how long were you there?"

"We started after sundown and I think we were there till about 11. We knew we had to leave before midnight when bad things happen."

"Did you ever see the guy with the machete?" Antonio asked.

"Once. I heard him threaten another man, threatened to cut off his arm if he was seen on his beach again."

"Can you tell me what he looked like?"

"He was about Orlando's height, how tall are you Orlando?" Francisco asked.

"I don't know, taller than you." Orlando muttered.

"Ok, I'll guess that you are about five foot eight inches." Antonio interrupted. "What else can you tell me?"

"He was thin, dark hair, wavy. It came down over his ears and covered his neck. He liked to show off his machete and couldn't wait to threaten people with it. Oh, and he had a dark tattoo on one of his arms. I couldn't see the shape well. I remember it was his left arm."

"That's a good memory, Francisco. Was it the upper part of his arm or the lower part?" Antonio asked as he remembered what Bianca had said about the man following her.

"The lower part, you could see it when he wielded the machete."

"He was holding the machete in his left hand? Are you sure?" Antonio continued his questions.

"Pretty sure, I remember thinking I would hold it in my other hand. It seemed unusual to me," Francisco said looking at his right arm for recall.

"That is great information Francisco. He was left handed with a tattoo on his lower arm. That will certainly make him easier to spot. Thank you. You've been very helpful."

"What will happen next? How long do we have to stay here?" asked Orlando.

"You should know that under article six of the Protection Conservation and Recovery of Sea Turtle Populations Law, sentences for sales of turtle eggs could get you three months to two years in jail if local law enforcement follows the law. I'll bet they'll just finish processing you and your arrest paperwork. You'll be fined and released by morning. Here's my card. Give me a call if you think of anything else, or if you see those men again." Antonio turned to walk away, pleased with the new information; the first real break in the case.

Chapter 25

Satisfied and full from their hamburgers, Daniela dropped Laura back at the condo. Laura was motivated to send the emails to her elected officials and contacted the media back home. She sent each a detailed letter about what happened and encouraged their support of Costa Rican conservation. She sent additional emails to *KTVU* in Oakland and *KSBU* out of Monterey. Soon after, a reporter from the Oakland station picked up the story and replied back. She hoped to set an appointment to speak with Laura via Skype and they scheduled a meet. Things were moving in the right direction and Laura went to bed satisfied. She'd taken the first step in bringing attention to the injustice that had occurred to her friends.

***

The phone alarm went off at 6 a.m., giving Laura an hour to get ready before Daniela's arrival at the condo for the trip to Cahuita. She moved swiftly through her morning routine donning the black A-line dress and gold necklace she purchased at the mall. Laura did a quick check of her email hoping for responses from congressmen and the media she contacted the night before forgetting she was on central time zone and California was still two hours behind her.

Googling "Gabriel Montenegro" pulled up new information reported by the media. The news wasn't just local anymore, information on his death had also been picked up by the *Huffington Post*, *National Geographic News Watch,* and the *New York Times*. She stumbled upon an entry to raise money for a memorial to Gabriel by a global project for the restoration of sea turtles and was amazed to see the support in donations worldwide went to help his family, build a memorial, and push the Costa Rican government to enforce current laws. It seemed her friend was leaving a legacy for the conservation movement around the world. This excited her and she couldn't wait to share it with Daniela.

Laura's cell phone rang.

"I'm outside," Daniela said.

"On my way," Laura closed the laptop, grabbed the umbrella, and locked the door as she headed out.

Alonso watched as the women left the complex. He followed, keeping a few cars between them. Once they hit route 32, he called Esteban to let him know they were on their way to Limón.

***

The rain was steady and the tat, tat, tat against the window woke Antonio. He took it as a sign to get an early start. He dressed in his standard uniform; a pair of Khaki pants and a white polo shirt with the OIJ logo on the left breast. He would head back to the Departamento de Policía de Limón to get the name of the individual from the security patrol he was determined to find. Then, he would follow up on the address he was given for one of the stolen cell phones.

"I'm Antonio De La Torres, the OIJ liaison from San José. We spoke on the phone the other day." Antonio reached his hand out to shake with Police Chief Gonzales. "We had spoken about the four men acting as security patrol the night of the Montenegro murder. I've been able to clear all but one individual. I understand you've received my supervisor's request for the name and address of the fourth policía. I'm eager to pursue questioning while I'm in the area."

"Very well, I did receive the request," responded Gonzales. "Manuel Jimenez Calderon is the man you want. He has been out sick this week."

"And do you think he is, or is he just avoiding questioning?"

"I've no reason to doubt him. He's a good man. I know he was upset about what happened to that biologist. He told me he felt powerless to stop them and hid himself."

"I see. Can you give me his address? I need to speak with him in person."

Gonzales's fat stubby fingers jotted the number and passed Antonio the slip of paper.

"Thank you. By the way, I understand that the security on the beach has been increased since this unfortunate death. What has the assignment been increased to?"

"We received orders from the MSP to increase it to 12 to cover several shifts throughout the day. Of course, this takes a number of policía off other posts in town. We have to wait for new recruits to finish training to reassign them to the vacated posts," Gonzalez said with displeasure.

"I thought that LSTC had pulled all volunteers from the shifts?"

"We're enforcing poaching laws but a few local volunteers continue to visit Playa Soledad."

"Too bad the MSP didn't direct you to have those 12 on shift prior to the murder." Antonio commented as he turned to leave.

***

Antonio pulled up to a small stereotypical Costa Rican square masonry home—two-bedroom, one bath, no front porch style in a rundown neighborhood. He knocked on the door then showed his badge to the lady who answered.

"I'm looking for Manuel Jimenez Calderon" Antonio said.

"He's not here," the lady replied. She had a youthful face, long black hair, and dark eyes.

"When do you expect him to return?"

"I don't know. He left a couple of days ago and I haven't heard from him," she said.

"I don't understand, the police chief said he was home ill."

"I know. He called his chief and then left. I don't know where he went," she said, worry crossing her face.

"And you are?"

"I'm sorry. I'm being rude. Please come in," she moved away from the door and directed him to the kitchen. "I'm his wife, Adriana. I'm concerned for him. It's not like him to take off and not call me. I haven't heard from him since he left."

"Why didn't you call the policía and report him missing?" Antonio said.

"I didn't want to get him in trouble for lying about being sick."

"Do you have any idea why he might have left?"

"After the death of that man on the beach, he was nervous. He was on patrol that night. He was worried someone would come after him."

"Did he see something that night? That's why I want to speak with him. I'm hoping he saw something."

"He didn't say anything to me. But he said he'd heard rumors about drugs being delivered near the beach he patrolled. He thought the death might be connected."

"I see," Antonio said, circling a word on his pad.

"Do you think he would have gone to San José or," he paused, "the Pacific coast? Does he know anyone he would go visit?"

"I don't think he went to San José. I don't know if he has friends outside of Limón. His parents had an old house near Siquirres, it has been abandoned about 10 years now. Maybe he went there. I think there was a lot of land around it based on the stories he told me."

"Have you tried calling him?"

"I've left messages on his cell phone, he hasn't returned them. I just pray he is hiding and will be ok until the people that killed that man are found."

Antonio grew concerned, "Has anyone else tried to contact him? Or stopped here to see him?"

"No, only you."

"Thank you for your time. Here's my card. If you hear from him, let me know. Let him know I can protect him."

Back at his car, Antonio called his office. He asked them to research addresses for any Jimenez's living in the Siquirres area currently and to look back ten years, mentioning the possible abandoned home. The cell phone research was next on his list.

***

Driving through the tiny town of Estrada thick with banana trees and a small population, Antonio came upon the little blue wooden shack with a corrugated metal roof and short square stilts that protected it from flooding and night creatures. A petite woman dressed in denim shorts and a purple tank top answered the door. Antonio went through the same badge routine, then asked, "Did you recently purchase a cell phone?" He recited the phone number.

"I received one as a birthday gift."

"And that was when?"

"Last Friday."

"Who gave it to you?" Antonio made more notes.

"My boyfriend."

"What is your boyfriend's name?"

"Pedro Villalobos Tres"

"Your name?"

"Susanna Martinez"

"Do you know where he purchased the phone?"

"No, he gave it to me as a gift. I didn't ask. Why?"

"The cell phone number you've been using was assigned to someone else who has reported it stolen."

"There must be some mistake," Susanna said.

"Is Señor Villalobos here? I would like to speak with him."

"He's working near Pocora, helping a friend move. He might be back tomorrow, but he wasn't sure how long it would take."

"I see. Do you have a phone number where I can reach him? I'll be heading toward Siquirres this afternoon, perhaps I can meet him there." said Antonio.

Susanna gave him the number.

"I'll need to take that phone as evidence since it has been reported stolen. Please hand it over." She did so with reluctance and he was on his way. He felt good about the developments today. Antonio called his office again and had them put a trace on the cell phone number for Pedro and requested a background check on Señor Villalobos Tres for prior arrests.

He left a message for Pedro but didn't expect he'd answer. He checked his watch and decided to stop for a quick lunch before the next location.

Susanna ran to her neighbors to use their phone and warn Pedro.

Chapter 26

Today was the day Gabriel would be buried. As Daniela and Laura made their way southeast to Limón Provence, Laura made small talk and asked Daniela about how her father met Gabriel's grandfather.

"My father was a student with a study project on green sea turtle nesting patterns in the Cahuita area. This was before it became a protected park in 1970. Gabriel's grandfather Victor was working there." She went on with Victor's history, and how Victor's idea led to many of the country's current national parks. Daniela's tone turned bitter when she continued, "It would seem that today all a foreign county has to do is dangle a large sum of money in exchange for a promise to develop something. The *Presidente* is not a popular one for this reason."

"Was Victor a conservationist at that time as well?" asked Laura.

"He was. He was a biologist like Gabriel. He also started with green sea turtles, then a few leatherbacks nested at Cahuita. That's when my father became interested. He worked at the Tortugero Nature Preserve for a while, specifically with leatherbacks. The two of them observed the nesting patterns and noticed a change- the turtles also nested along Playa Soledad. My father created the Leatherback Sea Turtle Conservancy from that information. His idea was to get volunteers to help watch nesting patterns, save the eggs, make studies on the health of the turtles. The Conservancy started at Tortugero and Victor helped with an added group at Cahuita, then they added Gandoca-Manzanillo Wildlife Refuge. Gabriel and I worked Playa Soledad because we saw more opportunity there. The other parks were more popular because they were on the tourist list. It's really Gabriel's dedication to Playa Soledad that has helped it grow."

"Did Gabriel's father play a part in LSTC also?" Laura adjusted her air vent.

"Victor's whole family was involved in the community and preserve at Cahuita. I don't think Gabriel had much of a choice, I think being a biologist was in his blood from a very early age. Ignacio, Gabriel's father, followed in the same footsteps. My father also worked with Ignacio at Cahuita. Ignacio would sometimes assist my father at Tortugero. Cahuita is really their home. Gabriel was a third generation conservationist. Ignacio still helps with tours of Cahuita when he can."

Changing the subject to the funeral, Laura had more questions. "Having never been to a funeral service in Costa Rica before, I'm assuming it's a Catholic mass. What should I expect?"

"Yes, there will be a mass at Iglesia Unidos En Cristo. Following that there is a funeral train where everyone walks behind the hearse to the Cementerio de Bribri. Expect that this will be very emotional, and all family, friends, and neighbors will be there. It's tradition in Costa Rica for the deceased to be buried the same day they died. However, because Gabriel was murdered it's a requirement that an autopsy be done." Daniela checked her rearview mirror and continued, "Formaldehyde is used when the process needs to be extended. Today's going to be difficult for those close to him because of the autopsy delay. His parents placed an obituary in *La Nación*, and the local television stations also scroll the obituaries to notify those outside of the family. A *Vela* is usually held the night before. Due to the delay, this didn't happen for Gabriel. At the cemetery, prepare yourself to see an above ground box tiled in white ceramic. They have a family plot and this is where his body will be placed sans the coffin."

Daniela added, "I wanted to leave early this morning because I want to stop at Playa Soledad to check on the hatchery and the security staff. They may have released a batch of eggs, I want to be sure they were tagged, but there are probably a couple more groups of eggs ready to release soon." Daniela saw a dark blue car a distance behind them in her rearview mirror. She thought the vehicle looked familiar. Probably one of the Limón business owners returning a day later.

***

The beach was quiet and desolate, no longer the activity hub it had been a week ago. A security guard stood near the hatchery and Daniela recognized a few of the local volunteers inside. She had cancelled the program on the beach, but was relieved to find a few people kept an eye out for hatchlings. As she pulled up to the side of the road to park, she saw the blue car again. She didn't see a front license plate and was disappointed she wasn't able to catch a number for Antonio.

"How's everything going?" Daniela asked the security guard as she walked to the hatchery.

"Pretty quiet, Tito and Gina stop by to check on the hatching progress. They predict approximately 80 eggs can be released in a week," he replied.

"That's great news," Laura chimed in. "Will we be coming back next week to see this? I would love to be a part of that."

"Sure, we could certainly use a positive event," Daniela replied.

The women only spent fifteen minutes on the beach.

A somber mood overtook them as they drew closer to Cahuita. As they approached the church, Laura was comforted to see a very large group of people dressed in black had come to pay their respects. She felt overwhelmed with this new experience, and took a couple of deep breaths to calm her anxiety. The women made their way to the front of the church and Daniela introduced Laura to Gabriel's parents. Laura saw Gabriel in his mother, and her heart broke for her. Daniela held back tears, but Laura knew they were close to the surface. Laura bit her lip to keep herself in control of her own emotions. Another hot, muggy, rainy day in the Caribbean. The combination of heat and solemnness made it a tough day.

They made their way into the church and took a seat in the pews a couple of rows behind Gabriel's parents. Laura caught a whiff of something pungent that made her think of pickles. A rather strong scent. She couldn't figure out what it was, but it made her sick to her stomach. She had heard formaldehyde could smell like that and Daniela had mentioned that it was used to preserve dead bodies.

She hoped it didn't come from the coffin. Maybe it was just on the clothes of the people from the mortuary.

The service took an hour and Laura couldn't wait to get outside. Between that smell and her sobs she had a headache. She needed fresh air. The last time she was this uncomfortable was the night she was kidnapped. Those thoughts crashed her memory, and her headache grew stronger. She had to step outside and find a quiet spot.

***

Alonso parked a block away and walked to the church. He wasn't wearing black like the majority of people paying their respects, but felt his drab dark blue shirt and jeans blended with the crowd. He was the age of many of Gabriel's friends and fit in. He would pay his respects with the rest of the mourners and keep an eye on Daniela and Laura.

***

The funeral train made its way along route 36, several cars following the hearse. Because of the rain, everyone decided to use their vehicles. Laura hadn't realized that Daniela was also nauseous. No sooner had they gotten into Daniela's Santa Fe heading for the cemetery, then she had to pull over to throw up. "Laura, I'm not feeling very well. Do you think that you would be able to take over and follow the cars to the cemetery?" Daniela said.

"Are you ok?" Laura sent a worried glance to her friend.

"Do you happen to have any aspirin on you? I have the worst headache. I'm not sure if it's because of the smell inside that church, the emotions, or a combination of both. This urge to keep getting sick isn't going help me drive."

"Sure. I can drive for you. I have a mild headache myself. There was a terrible smell in that church. I wondered if it was the formaldehyde you spoke about? I felt oppressive heat in there and so emotional. I thought it was just me but it looks like it affected you too. Here I'll take over, it'll be easy enough to follow everyone. Why don't you lie down in the back seat?" She suggested digging through her handbag for an aspirin.

"Thanks. I think I will."

***

Alonso followed at the back of the procession. After everyone parked he was able to walk up and peek into Daniela's Santa Fe. He saw Daniela, eyes closed, relieved she didn't see him. He continued at a slow pace up towards the cemetery as he stayed behind the crowd and kept his eye on Laura. At least that OIJ officer wasn't around.

He had contacted Esteban after the services to let him know that Laura was now in the driver's seat.

***

An additional hour lapsed before they were able to make their way back to San José. Daniela's head felt like spikes being hammered through it, and the hammering coincided with each heartbeat. They had to stop two more times for Daniela to vomit. Laura stopped to pick up a bottle of water for her in Limón, but even drinking water made her head pound.

They headed back to Heredia, Laura at the wheel. Fog had started to roll in. The two lane route 32 was wet, rainy, and what light there had been was now disappearing. Laura was dealing with fog and a sick Daniela. Her hands gripped the steering wheel tightly. *There sure are a lot of curves on this road*, she thought. With her driving senses heighted she approached the Zurqui Tunnel. With headlights on, she proceeded. *Boy its dark in here.* She could hear car horns blaring as others drove through. Keeping her eyes on the road ahead, lights came straight at her. Laura grabbed the steering wheel tighter—her breath was shallow, and her heart pounded. She swerved into the oncoming lane to avoid the car coming directly toward her, thankful for no traffic. After the car missed her by inches, she pulled back into her lane, hit a slick spot, and the SUV skidded into the wall of rock, shrub and wild grass ahead crunching the front end of Daniela's Santa Fe. "Oh my God! Daniela are you ok?" Laura frantic, turned to the back seat. Her legs felt numb.

"Yeah, hit my head against the driver seat and fell to the floor but otherwise ok. How about you?"

116

"I'm fine. A car came directly at us. I had to swerve to miss it. I'm so sorry I damaged your car. Should I call the policía or Antonio? We need to report that driver."

"I'd suggest you call Antonio. You don't have an actual Costa Rica driver's license. We don't want the policía involved if we can avoid it, they'll just use it as an opportunity to extort money out of you."

Laura found her phone, but her hands shook and she kept missing the numbers. It took three tries before she dialed Antonio.

"Antonio, we need help, there's been an accident."

"What's going on, where are you?" he said.

"I swerved to miss a car coming directly at me in the Zurqui Tunnel. I skidded and hit part of the embankment. We're on the side of the road. Daniela suggested I call you. She's been sick, so I was driving."

"Are there any witnesses?"

"No one has stopped or pulled over to see if we needed help. We're on our own. It's dark and foggy out here. Can you get here soon?" Laura felt panicky.

"Can you still drive the vehicle?"

"I don't know, I hope it's only dented, but in these conditions I can't get a good look. We need to get Daniela back to the condo. She's been vomiting since the funeral. I don't want to keep her out here. Should I wait for you? Drive back? Make a report? I don't know what I'm supposed to do?" Laura was pacing the length of the vehicle.

"I'll get there as quickly as I can. Stay in the SUV and keep your lights off, doors locked. I'll call when I'm closer and then you can signal me."

"Ok. Thank you. I'd feel better following you back to Daniela's place and I'll need your help getting her into the condo." Laura expelled a long sigh and jumped back into the driver's seat.

An hour passed before Antonio arrived. It was dark, the rain had started again, and the roads were deserted except for the three of them. Antonio grabbed a flashlight from his glove box and surveyed the front of the vehicle. "Looks like the front end is slightly damaged, you should be good to drive. I'll take an official report when we get to the condo, especially if you think someone was purposely trying to run you off the road. It might be connected to the other incident. I don't want to take any chances and will run with the assumption that it is," Antonio said.

"Whoever it was came awfully close. This could have been so much worse. We were lucky. Daniela's been vomiting and I think she's starting to get a fever. We need to get her into bed."

"Follow me."

Chapter 27

Once the rain stopped, fog again began to swirl around them as they drove back to Heredia. Laura could only see the yellow line in front of her and the two red dots of Antonio's tail lights. Back at the condo, Antonio helped walk Daniela to the door. Laura got her into bed, put a glass of water at the bedside table and put a cold washcloth on her forehead.

"Get a good night's sleep and hopefully the headache will be gone by morning. I'll sleep on the sofa tonight. Just let me know if you need anything," Laura said. They'd both been through quite an emotional day. Laura felt wrung out but was surprised at how hard the day seemed to hit Daniela. Antonio interrupted her thoughts.

"Did you see the car that was driving at you?" Antonio asked.

"No, just lights. The tunnel was really dark. Daniela had mentioned something about a dark blue Corolla she thought she had seen a couple of times. You should ask her about it if she feels better in the morning."

"I just need to fill out a few more things here and then I can leave you alone. You should also get some sleep."

"It's been quite a day. I don't know how much sleep I'll be able to get tonight. Thank you for coming and for helping us. You're the only one I felt comfortable calling."

"I'm glad I was able to help." Antonio lightly clasped his hands on hers.

***

Alonso checked in with Esteban and let him know that he was back on watch at the condo. He reported something had happened to Daniela since the OIJ official helped her to the door. He suspected Daniela would be staying at the condo for the night. "Good. Keep an eye on both of the women. Let me know if anything changes,"

Esteban hung up. After sitting in the car for over an hour, Antonio left. *Lights are off, it's still early, and I'm tired of being bored sitting here,* he thought. With no further movement to report, he contacted Pedro to see if he wanted to meet for drinks.

***

Esteban had the rest of the gang working at Pocora ranch. They were in the process of packing as directed by Wendigo. His last phone call, warned them to move faster. The helicopter had taken off with the final delivery to Nicaragua the previous day. Their task was to make the place look abandoned once more.

Finished, Esteban addressed the group. "Our shipments are now delayed due to your carelessness and the death of that biologist. Our priority is to get all equipment and belongings away from this ranch. We'll use Beni's van to bring supplies to storage. Wendigo and I are extremely angry that we've had to cut deliveries and lay low for the next six months. Your stupidity has cost us large sums of money and you'll feel it in your wallet. There will be limited work at the rafting operation, and you won't be able to count on that. You were paid generously for that last shipment, use it wisely."

After the meeting, Esteban stepped into a separate room to meet with each man individually. He pulled Luis aside. "Luis, hand me your machete," Esteban ordered.

"Why do you need my machete?" asked Luis.

"I understand you have been a very bad boy. It is not safe for you to play with such toys. Now, give me that machete," Esteban ordered in a firmer and louder tone. Luis reached to his side to get it and handed it to Esteban. "Luis, is it true that you are the one that stripped that man and tied him to the vehicle?" asked Esteban.

After a moment of silence, "Yes" he replied.

"And, is it true you drove his body through the sand?"

"Y-y-yes"

"*Que mierda* possessed you to do such a thing? You know Wendigo said no one was to be hurt."

"I...I was feeling powerful. I enjoyed scaring the hueveros on the beach, kidnapping those women. We are in control. It is our beach. No one can stop us. The biologist is dead. He can't stop us anymore." Luis felt a dose of confidence and stood straighter.

"I see," said Esteban. "Did you think the policía would not look for the killer? Did you not think that this would bring more security to the playa and postpone deliveries?" asked Esteban as his index finger gently surveyed the edges of the machete.

"No. The policía never enforce laws, I didn't think they'd investigate. I never thought it would postpone shipments."

"What do you think we should do about this error?" Esteban asked.

"I...I... don't know. I'm sorry. I didn't mean to hurt the business. It won't happen again." Luis softly stuttered as he looked at a crack in the cement floor.

"Am I to take your word for this, and believe you?"

"Yes. Yes. Please." Luis put his hands together in prayer form.

"Luis, I need you to sit down," Esteban motioned as he pulled out the chair.

Luis did so with a sense of dread. Esteban tied him to the chair. He placed each arm on the arm rest and tied each in place, he then paced the room as Luis sat there. Luis's eyes became huge and dilated, he was breathing heavier and his mouth was dry. He was afraid to speak and afraid to look at Esteban. Beads of sweat formed on his forehead and urine trickled down his pant leg as the smell of ammonia wafted up.

A few minutes passed before Esteban walked back to the table, picked up the machete, and played with it. He threw the tip of it into the table top and repeated the action a couple of times. Luis saw Esteban pick up the machete one more time, and before Luis could blink, Esteban had taken three of Luis's fingers off at the first knuckle joint. Blood spattered onto Esteban, seeped out of the fingers onto the arm of the chair, and dripped down to the floor. Luis let out a howling, blood curdling scream. His face became pale and he couldn't grab his other hand. He went into shock when he looked into Esteban's cold dark eyes. "Beni," Esteban called out.

"Yes. Sir," Beni responded quickly entering the room.

"You will need to get some bandages for Luis here. He hurt himself." Esteban ordered as he untied Luis. "Luis, see what happens when you play with a machete? You must be careful."

Beni helped Luis up from the chair, and they left to find a wrap for his hand.

"Sir," Beni came back to address Esteban. "Luis is bleeding through the cloth I gave him. With your permission, I would like to take him to a discreet clinic in Guapiles. I'll carry my Ruger for protection, but I'm confident we can plead stupidity with the machete. I'll put the supplies in the warehouse once we're done."

"Fine. You really need to harden that heart. Pedro can help me finish the small details and clean up the blood left behind. I'll have him burn the table and chairs before we leave." Esteban replied.

***

The next morning, Antonio headed back out and pulled into a roadside *Soda* near Siquirres. He was anxious to get a report from his office, and hated to wait. The investigation wasn't moving fast enough and he lacked information. He ordered the *plato del dia*, and tried the office again. His assistant answered the phone. "We have results for the rubber pieces found at the scene," he said.

"Great, that only took a week. What did they find?" Antonio asked.

"It's been confirmed that the rubber is the type used for inflatable boats. There were also small traces of a chemical with properties similar to cocaine."

"Well this should prove that drug trafficking is taking place on the north shore of Playa Soledad, but it doesn't prove that drugs were involved in the murder. Any luck with fingerprints?"

"I'm afraid not," the assistant answered.

"Ask the forensic team if they can do further research into the type of inflatable…could it be the type used in any of the local river rafting businesses, for example? Anything on the Siquirres search yet?"

"Nothing to report there, but Pedro Villalobos Tres had a previous arrest record for burglary and theft in Limón Province."

"So, it's possible he stole the cell phone his girlfriend used, but it doesn't necessarily connect him to the drugs or the murder," Antonio commented thinking out loud.

"You should also know that there have been several recent phone calls to the Siquirres Policía from residents near the Pocora area having seen a couple of helicopters flying over the rainforest. The residents reported it as suspicious because that activity isn't normal."

"Interesting." Antonio's curiosity was piqued. He checked his paperwork for the location of the second stolen cell phone. Near Siquirres. He decided to go to Pocora first then double back to Siquirres if necessary. He got the estimated location of the helicopter sightings and requested back up to meet him at the location in 30 minutes. He was getting excited now.

Antonio drove slowly along route 32 near Pocora watching for dirt roads or gaps in the jungle that might signal an encampment. He took a left on the first muddy road he came across and had to drive through standing water. He drove as far as he could, not seeing anything that looked like the area had been inhabited, when he received a call from the back up team.

They had taken another road and found that it led to a ranch. Antonio turned around to meet up with the other team. The second road, off route 32, was narrower but passable by vehicle. The road was muddy and rutted. They moved in and found two houses where construction wasn't completed. Antonio grabbed his .45 caliber Glock handgun. The law enforcement team slowly walked around the buildings signaling to each other. The place was empty.

They discovered rusted barrels that had been turned on their sides, a wheelbarrow turned over, and a pile of ash from what appeared to be a campfire. He could still smell the damp ash among the loam. There was a picnic table made of wood on the concrete slab under a roof, empty paper bags that had held white powder. They found no one; no vehicles, no equipment recently used. Antonio walked, gun up, going from room to room. He saw droplets of what he thought might be blood on the floor in one of the rooms. There wasn't a lot, but he hoped there might be enough to collect some DNA. One of the other officers pointed out the path that led to the makeshift helicopter pad.

This was the place, it looked like drugs had been processed here, but the question was how recently? Antonio made a call and requested a crew from the Department of Forensic Science. He took pictures, but the forensic team would need to check for prints and test the powder from the bags. Antonio hoped it would tell what activity went on here. It would be at least another week for results, two if DNA was possible from the blood. Still no one to question.

A third officer searched the second house and found an AK-47 under one of the three sets of bunk beds. The beds were skeletons, no mattresses or bedding so the investigators weren't sure how recently they had been used. Antonio thought to himself, *definitely one individual here, with the amount of beds, could be up to six.* He was confident three people were involved, and it would make sense that there needed to be at least five to kidnap everyone that night. "This could be a connection to the kidnappings. Let's hope there are prints on those beds," Antonio said.

He also requested a team from the drug enforcement department to act as guards for the site. Perhaps their knowledge would help with the forensics needed. *¡Maldita sea!* Antonio said to himself disappointed that the place was abandoned. Not as promising as he'd wanted.

He called the office to follow up on the search for Jimenez parties in Siquirres. Time had moved fast; he couldn't believe his watch read 3 p.m. *I'll need to spend another night out. ¡Mierda!* He asked if Pedro's phone had been traced. Was he in the area near where it had been used?

Chapter 28

Pedro stood next to Alonso at a bar in Guapiles after he completed the Pocora move. "Alonso, man, you have got some bad breath. Get away from me, it smells like something died inside you. And, when was the last time you showered? You stink."

"I'm sorry, I have a bad tooth. The coke sometimes helps with the pain, let's get something to drink, I need to numb it again." Alonso ordered a *Guaro*.

"*Mae*, go see a dentist and get that thing removed."

"What do I do about the OIJ guy calling about the phone? Do I tell him I found it? I'm sure Esteban would kill me if finds out I gave a phone to Susanna." Pedro said.

"That's what I would say. He probably knows you've got a record for theft already. I hope you cleaned everything that was on that phone," Alsonso responded.

Pedro sipped his tequila. "I deleted everything before I gave it to her."

"*Mae*, someone is still being charged for that phone number. You need to replace the SIM card. Someone will track it down eventually. Get rid of it. Make up some story to Susanna, but don't let her use it anymore. Esteban will hurt you, he doesn't like mistakes."

Alonso thought of the phone *he* kept. He had tested it once, and at his house. He too could be in trouble if someone found it. He needed to destroy it as soon as possible. He would head home, hope there was no activity at the condo, because he wasn't where he was supposed to be.

"Susanna said she told the officer I would be home tomorrow. Do you think if I don't call him back he'll be waiting for me to show up?" Pedro asked.

"Don't freak out," Alonso swirled the *guaro* in his glass, "Stay cool, tell him you bought it and will take it back. Say you didn't realize the guy you bought it from had stolen goods. Keep it simple. Let him wait for you. Let him know you didn't get a message. You know cell phone service is sketchy in some locations. That excuse is completely believable."

Pedro groaned at the *fútbol* game on the bar's TV as his favorite player was called offsides.

"It looks like we're done with the shipments and batches for a while. Do you think Esteban will give us work at the rafting company?" Pedro asked.

"I don't know. It's not peak tourist season, maybe he'll have odd chores. I would be careful with the money we earned just in case he doesn't. We need to lay low for a while." Alonso answered.

Daniela had a rough night and could barely sleep. Her headache was worse than any migraine she had ever suffered. Walking to the bathroom made her head feel like a bomb was exploding within it. She was thankful the vomiting had stopped but now she was getting the chills. Laura tiptoed in to the bedroom.

"How are you feeling?" she asked.

"I've never felt such pain in my head. I barely slept. Even drinking water is uncomfortable. My eyeballs hurt. I'm freezing. I think I have a fever. This has got to be the flu. My body aches, and my lower back hurts. It feels like someone is sticking knitting needles in me. I'm not going to be able to get any work done today," Daniela said.

"I'll do as much as I can for you. Anything I can do to make you more comfortable?" Laura adjusted the temperature on the air conditioning as she knew not to bury a fever in blankets. She saw that Daniela had been drenched in sweat.

"You look flush. I poured you some more water and a glass of mango juice. Here," Laura handed the glass to Daniela and put the back of her hand to Daniela's forehead. "You're definitely burning up. Let me find the thermometer." She took Daniela's temperature—103 degrees. "You have a fever. It'll be important to keep drinking liquids. You don't want to get dehydrated."

"I'm sure I'll be fine tomorrow. I rarely get fevers and when I do, they usually only last a day. I need to be in Limón in two days" Daniela said.

"Oh, what's going on?" Laura asked.

"MINAE and MSP will be in Limón to tell people about Gabriel's murder and other security issues. I'm going to be a thorn in the side of Senior Rodriguez. Also, there should be another group of hatchlings ready to head to sea so I want to make sure that happens."

"Well then you better get some sleep. Maybe you can sweat out this fever. Can I get into your laptop? I can take over and finish some of the work you started while you rest, if that will help." Laura said.

"Sure, I'd appreciate it if you went into the MINAE file, my most recent document needs to be edited, it would help if you could do that. I started writing a speech for the Limón visit, look that over and let me know what you think." Daniela said as she closed her eyes.

Chapter 29

On his way to Siquirres, Antonio answered a call regarding the Jimenez family he'd been waiting for. A family with that name had resided in the area ten years previous. "I'm not sure this is what you are looking for," said the assistant. "This Jimenez family owned a farmhouse north east of the Pacuare River. It seems an earthquake damaged it some years back and they left it abandoned. Banco De Costa Rica owns the property now and has the land up for sale. There hasn't been much activity in real estate in that area though, so it's probably been vacant this entire time. With any luck, there will be a for sale sign in the area."

"Thank you. I'll check it out, it's the only thing we have at the moment," Antonio said.

Putting his four-wheel drive in gear, Antonio crossed the rugged dirt, rock and grass paths that led to the farmland in the area. Although he'd taken good care of his vehicle, he'd created a mess, slathered in mud from the rains and the roads he'd driven from Limón. He adjusted the air conditioning vents to hit his face.

The population in Siqurres consisted of tourists staying at a nearby lodge with reservations for river rafting tours. He drove slowly, eyeing places where someone could hide, like abandoned casas. The forest had been cleared for pasture, but a few spindly trees survived. He drove around for 30 minutes when he came upon the remnants of a wooden pole and post fence that seemed to outline a property. Some of the poles had fallen. Brahma cows roamed free and the scent of manure permeated the truck.

Antonio glimpsed a cluster of palm trees and something pink in the distance. As he moved closer, he saw an abandoned masonry farmhouse painted carnation pink supported by greyed and weathered poles. Windows were reclaimed tree limbs and were missing glass and screens. Cracks were running up the side of one

Murder in Costa Rica

of the walls. There was no door just an opening. Antonio got out of the truck and called Manuel's name. No answer. He stopped to listen for noises. Quiet. He saw several stained spots on the concrete floor. Yellow-brown Pharaoh ants were on the walls and crawling over warped window sills.

He took his Glock from his waist and walked through the house with it in front of him. A lime green snake with darker markings was coiled in a corner. *Parrot snake?* Antonio wasn't sure if it was poisonous or not, and wouldn't get close enough to find out. There were holes in the wall where a kitchen had once been. The house smelled musty with a hint of animal feces. With gun in front of him, each room was cleared before he entered. One room contained thin green blankets that looked relatively fresh. Someone slept there recently.

No one was in the house. Antonio moved to the back and found an old black beat up and rusted muscle car parked under a palm tree. Someone was here, where were they hiding? He looked into the car, bent to look under it. The trunk was closed, tires inflated, no cobwebs. There were tire tracks in the mud-grass-soil blend beyond it, so it had been driven recently. There were no other buildings nearby.

Antonio searched the ground for footprints and looked to a stand of trees to the southeast of him, about a quarter mile away. The Pacuare River was beyond that.

He maneuvered through the trees looking around and up to see if he could find a camp or hiding spot. The ground was covered in loose gravel and difficult to discern footprints. Antonio slowed behind each tree, surveyed the area and headed toward the water in hopes of seeing footprints in the muddy soil there.

As he approached the riverbank, he thought he saw movement to his left. He stopped and turned. A piece of rust colored fabric poked out from behind a tree. He called out "Manuel Jimenez?" The man fled north. Antonio ran after him.

"Manuel, I just want to speak with you. I'm Antonio De La Torres. I am an investigator with the OIJ. Please. I just want to talk. I can protect you," he shouted as he pursued the man. Antonio glimpsed a bald head. It had to be Manuel. He thought he was chasing a frightened man from the *Policía de Limón*, until it

129

registered that this person fit the description Orlando gave him for one of the men at beach. Antonio was faster and was able to tackle the man just as they were emerging from the tree line.

"Are you Manuel Jimenez?" asked Antonio.

"Sí," Manuel panted in reply.

"Are you an officer of the Policía de Limón?"

"Sí."

"I need to speak with you regarding the death of Gabriel Montenegro. I understand you were part of the security patrol that night."

"Yes, I was, I can't speak with you, they'll kill me."

Antonio got up from the ground then helped Manuel.

"Who are 'they'?" Antonio asked.

"The drug smugglers, I think they saw me. I saw what they did. They will do the same to me." Manuel pleaded.

"Tell me what you saw. I can protect you. I spoke with your *Jefe*, he said you told him you were outnumbered and overpowered so you ran away. Is that true?"

"Sí."

"Then you have nothing to be afraid of, we can protect you and your family until we catch them and bring them to trial. Your *Jefe* tells me you've been dependable. This will help you," Antonio added.

"You don't understand. I know them. I know who killed that man. They've threatened to kill my wife if I say anything," Manuel said, his muscles tensed, his throat dry.

Antonio stood motionless and recognized Manuel's fear. This was information not expected.

"You were a part of them, weren't you?" asked Antonio, "Were you taking payoffs to stay quiet about the drugs?"

"Something like that." Manuel said shrugging his shoulders.

"Tell me about it."

"I want to know how you can protect me and my wife first. She doesn't know about this, I don't want them to come after her," said Manuel.

"We have a Witness Protection Program. It would mean that you and your wife would have to leave the country, start over, but you would be alive. We would need your testimony at trial in exchange for the protection. I was able to find you. It's only a matter of time before they will."

"I told them I was going away so I wouldn't have to speak with you. I assured them my wife doesn't know anything."

"How long do you think you can stay away before they will be looking for you? Your wife is in a vulnerable position. All they have to do is get to her and they know you will come out of hiding."

"They don't know where we live." Manuel wiped away sweat from his forehead.

"Come on," Antonio said, "I was able to use my resources to track you down. You think they don't have the same kind of resources. You took a bribe, what makes you think there isn't someone else who won't take one?"

"If I agree to protection, where would we go? Can our family come with us?"

"We could put you in Nicaragua, Panama, Honduras, or Guatemala. The culture and language would be similar, but your names would be different. And, no it would only be your immediate family, it would be best to leave and not let anyone know where you are. Any family members that would know jeopardize their safety as well as yours."

"But what about my job? It doesn't pay much but it is a respectable job."

"Word gets out that you're policía on the take, you won't even have that. We'll set you up with a new identity give you a place to stay and a new job. I've seen where you live, it would be nicer accommodations."

"How do you know they won't get to me first if I testify at the trial?"

"We don't. We will have officers on security for you when you return for the trial. It will be like having multiple body guards. You pass on the offer they'll get to you eventually. If you get arrested, they'll come after you in jail. Refuse the offer, and I can arrest you right now for obstruction and taking payoffs. It's your choice."

"Say I take the offer, when would we leave, and how can you be sure the people you work with can be trusted?"

"I work with a select few in this type of situation. I would put my life in their hands. I can give them a call once we talk, and they can start making the arrangements. It would be best if you left tonight, there is no time to waste."

"Ok, I'll talk to you. I want you to come with me to explain this to my wife and know that you are protecting us while we pack our things."

As they walked back to the farm house, Manuel told him the story and explained why he took the incentives.

"I didn't expect anyone to be killed. I was to help unload agricultural products, I needed an easy way to earn money to support my wife. I learned that Wendigo is the one calling the shots and he is very rich and lives in Columbia."

Manuel continued, "The more deliveries I helped with the more dangerous it seemed to become. I didn't try to stop them that night because two of the men were on drugs and acting crazy and I thought I could get hurt. I just wanted to get the shipment into the van and get to the ranch then disappear."

"This ranch, where is it located?" Antonio asked

"In Pocora."

Antonio knew he needed more evidence than the word of one witness. He would need the investigative work to back it up, and others would have to corroborate the story. Manuel told him about the ranch in Pocora and, if the crime investigation team was thorough, there could be evidence to back the arrests. He gave up the names of the others. Antonio would start the background process on them. He hoped to bring them all in at once, so word of arrests wouldn't leak to the others.

Chapter 30

After a second night in Limón, Antonio drove to Estrada to speak with Pedro. He'd sit in his car and wait for Pedro to return if he had to. Thanks to Manuel, he knew Pedro was part of the group. He would only question him about the stolen cell phone as was his initial plan and wing it from there. He arrived at the Villalobos Tres residence around 8 a.m. and sat in his truck across the street waiting for activity.

***

Daniela managed to sleep in four-hour increments but awoke, drenched from fever. The air conditioning had been turned off so she wouldn't chill further. Daylight became night and Laura got through the stagnant heat by opening the sliding door and turning on the ceiling fan.

The next morning Daniela said "I'm going to take a shower, and change my night clothes. I've been sweating a lot. Everything's damp." She took a short but taxing walk to the bathroom. Her skin was so sensitive the spray from the shower felt like tiny BB's pelting her. Her bones still ached and the fever hadn't broken.

"I changed the sheets while you were in the shower. Everything's fresh. How are you feeling, did the shower help?" asked Laura.

"I'm afraid not, everything hurts. My bones. My skin. My head. I'm even having weird dreams."

"You're not drinking very much water or juice either. Do you think you could eat something? You need to build your strength if you're going to make that Limón meeting," Laura scolded.

"I'm not hungry. I'll try some water, but my head throbs with every sip. I'm just so uncomfortable and feel so weak, unfocused." As she nestled back into bed and pulled the coverlet up to her neck,

Daniela said, "Has Antonio tried to call? Any news regarding the investigation?"

"I talked with him briefly last night. He was going to speak with the other security patrol officer and had leads on a couple of the cell phone numbers. He also spoke to the two hueveros that you and Gabriel knew. They gave him a description of three guys. He was optimistic about the information." Laura sat on the corner of the bed, "The *Tico Times* reported two speed boats loaded with cocaine were seized in the Caribbean near Playa Soledad. I don't know if it's connected to Gabriel's murder, but it does confirm what he suspected." Laura placed a cold cloth on Daniela's forehead.

***

Antonio grabbed a cup of coffee and a banana as he left the hotel. He sat in his truck, eyes on the Villalobo Tres residence, sipping the warm liquid. He'd waited for about an hour when a yellow battered subcompact pulled up. Once the man entered the house, Antonio went to the door and Pedro answered. "Pedro Villalobos Tres?" Antonio asked the man with dreadlocks, pencil thin mustache and closely trimmed goatee.

"Who's asking?" replied Pedro. Antonio introduced himself with the badge and credentials routine.

"Susanna told me you would be back. How can I help you?" Pedro's tone was stern.

"Your girlfriend was in possession of a stolen phone. She said she received it as a birthday gift from you. Is that correct?" Antonio asked.

"Yes," said Pedro.

"Where did you get it?"

"I bought it from one of the phone places on Market Street in Limón about a week ago, I think."

"Do you remember, was it a Kolbe/Ice location for example? Or the name of the individual that sold it to you?" Antonio looked past Pedro to scope out the home.

"No. I was in the area visiting some friends watching a fútbol game at a bar. I went to a small stand near Parque Vargas. I remembered that I better get a gift while I was in town and happened to be near the street vendors."

"Did you purchase the phone from a man or woman? And, can you describe them?"

"A man, no description, I didn't really pay attention. I needed to pick up a cheap phone and head back home. I didn't want all the paperwork hassle you get at one of the stores." Pedro looked bored with the conversation.

"I see."

"Look, I'll take it back. I'll let them know they sold me a bad phone, hopefully they'll give me a new one for the trouble."

"This meeting with your friends in Limón, do you remember what day that was?"

"End of the week, Thursday or Friday."

"Which game were you watching?" Antonio asked hoping this would help identify a specific evening.

"Our national team was playing Canada. I don't remember dates."

"Can you give me the names of the friends that you were with? The name of the bartender? I need to confirm this information."

"Why do you need this information? What difference does it make? I purchased a phone that I didn't know was stolen," Pedro adopted a defensive attitude.

"Mr. Villalobos, the phone you gave as a gift was stolen. You have a prior arrest for theft, so I'm having a hard time believing you purchased it. Also, a police report related to the phone was made by a foreigner who was kidnapped last week. We need to confirm your whereabouts or I'm afraid you'll be a suspect in that kidnapping." Antonio said.

"All right, I'll give you the names," Pedro acquiesced making up most of the names.

"Mr. Villalobos, I will also need their contact information."

Antonio didn't believe for a minute that Pedro was being honest with him. He would go through the motions to see if any of the names came up in a search and if anyone could vouch for Pedro and would be looking into the fútbol schedule.

"One more thing, I have that phone in my possession as evidence. I wouldn't leave town if I were you," Antonio headed back to his truck. He called the new information into his office and headed back to Siquirres to question the second cell phone location.

Chapter 31

Driving through the main square and around the fútbol field, Antonio came to a lime green house with a red roof surrounded by dirt and a chain link fence. This was the address for cell phone number two. A middle-aged woman answered the door. Following introductions, he said he knew a stolen cell phone was tracked to this address. *"No posible,"* said the woman, *"sin telefono aqui* we go into town to make calls."

"Does anyone else live here with you?"

"Sí, mi esposo y mi hijo."

"Any recent guests who had a phone with them?" He looked bewildered and double checked the address to his notes.

"No," she answered.

"What about your son? Is he here can I speak with him?"

"Alonso" the woman called out. A young man about 20 peeked his head out of his bedroom door and the woman motioned him over. "This is my son, Alonso."

Antonio made note of his dark wavy hair, lighter skin, blue eyes, bushy eyebrows, and a strong odor emanating from him. *Strong odor, halitosis? Laura mentioned a strong odor* Antonio thought to himself. When questioned about the phone, Alonso said, "I do have a cell phone, I purchased it in Guapiles a couple of months ago. Here. Take a look, I'm sure this isn't the one you're looking for." He handed the phone to Antonio who pulled up the number and compared it to his notes. It didn't match.

"Could someone have used a phone near here? asked Alonso.

"Doubtful." Antonio continued his questioning. "Do you know a Pedro Villalobos Tres?"

"No." Alonso said thinking *shit, he spoke to Pedro.*

"I see. Well, Señor Villalobos gave me your name, said you were watching a fútbol game together."

"Oh?" he paused, "yeah, I met a group of guys in Limón one night. I didn't get a last name. We watched the fútbol game at the bar."

"What night was that exactly?"

"I'm pretty sure it was Thursday or Friday, about a week ago." Alonso tapped his foot nervously against the base of the door.

"Was this the Nationals playing Canada by chance?"

"Yes. Crazy night, lots of locos."

"Did you know Señor Villalobos was in possession of a stolen cell phone? I find it interesting that you two are friends. We have two stolen cell phones and each of your addresses is linked to them. Coincidence?" asked Antonio.

"I can honestly tell you, I don't have the cell phone you're talking about. Feel free to search the house. I have nothing to hide." Alonso said, stepping aside and casting a smug look to Antonio.

"Thank you. I will." Antonio moved forward noticing the strong vinegar smell of the ceviche the woman had been making.

Antonio didn't find the phone, but confirmed Alonso knew Pedro. Alonso became suspect number four. Guilt by association. Alonso was also a name Manuel gave him. Circumstantial? Maybe. Walking back to his truck, Antonio checked the garbage cans on the side of the house. Nothing. He called his supervisor with his suspicions. He was going to need more help locating and searching trash recently taken from this location. It could have been tossed elsewhere, but they would start here. *Dead end* Antonio cursed to himself. He had four suspects, one in a witness protection program, and no significant evidence for arrests.

***

Laura checked on Daniela several times. She was still feverish, yelling out in her sleep. Laura was torn. She knew Daniela's illness was escalating and didn't want to leave her alone but knew she better get to Limón if she was going to help with MINAE. She was determined to step in Daniela's shoes and not miss a beat in this fight.

She phoned Antonio. "Are you still in Limón?"

"Just got back to San José, several things to follow up on here. Why? What's going on?"

"I'm going to Limón to catch the MINAE and MSP speech. Daniela's still ill, seems to be getting worse and I hate to leave her alone. She thinks it's the flu, but I'm not so sure. I know she wouldn't want to miss this opportunity with MINAE. I don't know what to do. I know you're busy with the investigation but I didn't know who else to call. I need to find someone that could check on her while I'm gone. I need to leave within the hour."

"Well," Antonio glanced at his watch, "I can check on her around lunchtime, will that work?

"Yes, thank you."

"Let her know to call me if she needs anything. I may have to visit Limón and Siquirres again but I'm available for the day."

"I'll put a key under the doormat, I doubt she'll hear you knock."

Laura woke Daniela to let her know she was leaving. Daniela was too tired to argue. "Call 911 if you need help. The phone's here on the night stand. Antonio's in town, call him if you need anything. He'll stop by around lunch time to check on you. I know how important these meetings are to you, you've taught me that we have to stay on top of developments with MINAE."

"I'll be fine." Daniela mumbled and closed her eyes.

"I put a small plate of crackers, and a banana on the bedside. Your water's right here." Laura set the glass down on the table and turned to leave.

***

Alonso left Siquirres and made it back to the condo just as Laura was leaving. He dialed Esteban. "The blonde woman left the condo and she's alone. The Segura woman is still inside. Do you want me to follow her or stay put?" he asked.

"See if you can determine which direction she's going. Stay on the line with me as you follow her," Esteban said.

Alonso pulled out slowly and followed her as she came around the bend in Daniela's dented Santa Fe. He followed until she merged onto route 32 going southwest. "It appears she's heading back to Limón."

"Go watch the condo. I'm in Guapiles, I'll watch for her to come through and pick up the tail." said Esteban.

***

Alonso drove back to his spot and parked. The rain pelted his window as he played *Angry Birds* to relive boredom. Another hour ticked by, no movement. *This would be a good opportunity to sneak in. If she's sick, she won't be able to fight back. Let's have some fun.*

He left his car and sloshed through the puddles in the rutted road to the front door. He placed his ear against the door. No television or music was playing. He knocked and wedged his shoulder to push his way in if she opened the door. The element of surprise was his.

No answer. Alonso picked the lock and entered. The strips of greyed light peeking between vertical blinds was the only illumination. He closed the door quietly and listened. No movement. A laptop was on the island. He turned it on. The websites for *OIJ*, *MINAE*, the *Tico Times* and some sea turtle organizations were all saved in the drop down menu. There was no open email. He crept to the bedroom, looked around the corner and saw her asleep. He stood and watched her. She was pale and breathing heavy. He moved forward and climbed astride her on the bed.

Daniela woke in a fuzz, everything was a blur. She tried to scream but no noise came out. She tried to kick, but he was sitting on her, her arms and legs pinned against the mattress. She kept trying to scream but only managed a whimper.

***

Caught in the late morning deluge, Antonio pulled up to the condo around noon, made his way to the front door and knocked. No answer. He called for Daniela and identified himself. Alonso heard the knock, then "Daniela, are you there? It's Antonio." He sprang from the bed and sprinted to the terrace. He opened the glass sliding door, slid out and backed into a thick thorn from the corner fuchsia bougainvillea bush. He moved to the wrought iron terrace railing, leapt to the side street below, rolled into the mud and ran to the car. With no movement from within, Antonio found the key under the mat.

***

Antonio realized the door was already unlocked. He was sure Laura said she locked it. Once inside, he saw the sliding door ajar. The clamminess outside seeped into the room bringing with it the wet smell of concrete. He heard the AC click on. *That's odd*, he thought.

He made a mental note to check with both women about the open door. He called Daniela again, and heard babbling coming from the bedroom. He rushed toward it and found her drenched in sweat with a red measles-like rash covering her chest. She tried to speak but words were slurred. "Daniela, it's Antonio. I'm here to help you," he said.

Her eyes were wide in fright, and she didn't recognize him. "Who, who are you? Why are you here?" Her words were thin, airy.

"Daniela, it's Antonio. Remember me? Laura told you I'd be by to check on you." He tried to reassure. "I'm here to help. How are you feeling?" he asked.

"Where am I?" she mumbled trying to sit up.

"You're home. You've been ill. You look very weak; I'm concerned about you." Antonio touched her forehead and checked her pulse, weak. He knew the rash and red palms were signs of Dengue fever.

"Daniela, I'm taking you to the emergency room. You're very warm and you have a rash."

"What's on me? Something is crawling on me." She started frantically scratching herself.

Antonio grabbed her arms, looked her in the eyes. "Daniela, listen to me. There's nothing on you, but I think you're very sick. I need to get you to the emergency room. They can help you with the itching and the fever. Stay with me. I want to help you," he said trying to calm and reassure her while he brushed back damp hair from her face.

Chapter 32

Antonio decided it would be faster to bring her to the emergency himself than wait for the Red Cross volunteer ambulance service to send one. He carried her limp body to his truck. Her hair was tousled and matted from sweat. Hospital San Vincente de Paul was ten-minutes away.

At the emergency room entrance, Antonio ran inside shouting for help. An attendant came out with a gurney and moved quickly to get her inside.

A nurse took her blood pressure, pulse and temperature, and questioned Antonio.

"I think she's been sick for about three days. I went to check on her and this is what I saw. Her roommate was concerned that the fever and the pain she was complaining about might be something other than the flu. She didn't say anything about the rash or the red palms. I think that's new. She was very hot to the touch so I rushed her here. She didn't recognize me and was confused and slurring her words when I asked her questions. I know the rash, slurring, and high temperatures can all be part of Dengue. News reports have mentioned cases have increased this year, so I wanted to get her here quickly."

"Thank you," said the nurse. "The doctor will be here soon. Can you stay with her until he gets here?"

"Sí," Antonio replied.

"I'll get some cool damp wraps on her to bring the fever down," said the nurse.

"She was complaining of itching, said something was crawling on her, and she started scratching herself." He looked at the nurse with concern. "Will the wraps help that?"

"No, but they'll cool her temperature and keep her from scratching in the short term, I'll apply some hydrocortisone cream to the rash to relieve the itching while I get the wraps ready." She touched Antonio's arm to reassure him.

The doctor arrived, read the nurse's notes, examined Daniela's rash and palms of her hands and the base of her feet. The doctor looked up from his patient to Antonio. "I understand you think she has contracted Dengue fever."

"Sí."

"The rash, the fever, the red palms certainly suggest that's the case. We'll give her some acetaminophen to help her pain and aid in bringing the fever down, then start an IV to help rehydrate her. Has she been able to eat or drink much?"

"I'm not sure, I can call her friend and let you know. Her friend said she had been sleeping most of the time," Antonio pulled his phone from his pocket.

"We'll get that IV started. We'll need to keep her overnight and possibly a couple of days."

Antonio walked outside. The rain and fresh air revived him. He called Laura. She didn't answer so he left a message telling her Daniela was at the hospital and would be staying overnight. He left his number and hoped she would contact him soon.

***

Alonso made it back to his vehicle and caught his breath. His knees hurt from the jump and the pressure to the bottom of his feet made them burn, but he was sure he hadn't been seen. The OIJ official carried the brunette out in his arms, her head limp like a rag doll. Alonso grabbed his water bottle and took a swig before putting the car in gear. Once Antonio's truck passed him, he followed. At the hospital, he pulled into a parking spot that allowed him to keep an eye on the emergency entrance.

He saw Antonio run in and then come back out with a hospital worker and a gurney. It seemed like an hour passed before he saw the OIJ man step outside again, this time to make a phone call. Alonso had a feeling he would be here a while. Time to contact Esteban again. He would sit until further instructions were received.

***

Laura arrived in Limón around 10 in the morning, as a crowd started to gather on the street in front of the bright turquoise blue Prosecutor's building. A volunteer was busy setting up a podium and microphone. The MINAE meeting was scheduled to take place there. The sky was gray with menacing clouds above, but no rain. The wind whipped up just enough sand from the streets to create a dust devil. She discerned a smell of curry, rice, and beans floating on the air.

Rafael Rodriguez was expected to meet privately with Gabriel's parents before he addressed the crowd. Laura was pleased to see locals arrive with protest signs once more, saying "Viva Gabriel", "Proteger Nuestras Playas" (protect our beaches), and "Proteger Nuestras Negocios" (protect our businesses).

She saw Gabriel's parents arrive and quickly went to meet them giving each a hug and letting them know they had her and Daniela's support. They thanked her and made their way to their meeting with Señor Rodriguez. Laura grabbed a spot up front near the podium and was determined to stand there for a couple of hours if she had to.

The Minister of Environment and the MSP emerged from the building at noon. Rafael stepped to the podium to address the small crowd. He was more casual this time, dressed in a starched white button down shirt and khaki twill pants. His hair slicked back. He still reminded Laura of a slimy salesman.

"We have come here today to meet with the prosecutor, National Police and regional OIJ regarding the murder of Gabriel Montenegro. We understand that media coverage of this event has also affected your local businesses. We have been assured that this case is being taken seriously.

"The investigation is in its early stages and there is much information to review and new information is coming to light each day. We have a couple of suspects, but not enough evidence to make arrests. We understand the reward for information and conviction regarding this murder has increased to $60,000." Rafael adjusted the mic.

"We have taken action to increase security surrounding Playa Soledad, and have agreed to create lookout posts that will be manned by the National Police in the Tortugero National Forest. We understand the urgency to improve the security infrastructure in Limón Provence.

"Several proposals are in review that could include co-management of areas within Playa Soledad and the wetlands adjacent. This proposal would collaborate with local fishermen and the community. The Costa Rican Coast Guard has been brought back to patrol the Caribbean seas, along with continued support of the United States Navy. Just last night the Coast Guard stopped a semi-submersible near the port of Limón. They confiscated seven tons of cocaine. These are immediate actions we have taken to resolve the unfortunate situation that occurred almost two weeks ago."

In a surge of courage, Laura shouted out in Spanish: "What action have you taken to make Playa Soledad a national park? The nesting patterns of the leatherback sea turtle have changed and this playa has become more important to the survival of the species. When will this be done?"

"This is a proposal we are taking under consideration. We need to conduct a feasibility study as there is pending residential development in the area as well as plans for an expansion of the port being financed by our partners from China. We appreciate everyone's interest in resolving this matter and appreciate your support. We will meet again at the MINAE offices in San José on 18 June. We hope to have arrests at that time. Thank you." Rafael concluded and walked back into the building.

The crowd started to disburse. Laura never saw the sporty red Jeep that had tailed her from Guapiles and didn't know Esteban was in the crowd. She made her way back to Daniela's SUV and checked the message from Antonio on her phone. "What's going on? I just got your message. What happened? Why's she in the hospital?" Laura spoke rapidly running her fingers through her hair nervously.

"Laura, calm down. I got to the condo and she was developing a rash. She was very weak and her temperature was still climbing. She didn't recognize me and was slurring her words so I brought her to the emergency room. They're trying to bring her fever down now and have given her an IV to rehydrate her. She is stable and under observation, but she'll have to stay overnight, and probably a couple of days according to the doctor." Antonio paced the halls as he spoke.

"I don't think she had eaten much. She had some mango juice, mostly water. I set out crackers and a banana when I left."

"Those were still on the bedside table when I got there. Now that I think of it, the light on the laptop screen was on and the patio door was open. Is that how you left everything this morning?"

"No. The laptop was off. I shut and locked the sliding door. I'm sure of it. I turned the air conditioning on low before I left. Do you think someone was in there?"

"I don't know, Daniela could have gotten up and opened it, but she was so weak when I saw her that I doubt that's the case. I'll ask her about it when she's more alert."

"I'm going to stop at the hatchery at Playa Soledad. Daniela had mentioned that hatchlings were ready to be released. I'll check on the status of that and see if there are any volunteers that can give me an update. I hope so, cause I'm not sure what I should do if the hatchlings are ready. I'll be on my way back after that. Should I come straight to the hospital? Is she in a room yet? Will you be there?"

"She is not in a room yet. I'll stay until you get here. I can't do much more on the investigation until Monday anyway. I need to follow up on some forensic evidence."

"Señor Rodriguez, when he addressed the townspeople in Limón today, said there were two suspects and he hoped there would be an arrest by the 18th. Is that true?" Laura needed to pin down some information.

"Uh, not exactly. I do have suspects, more than two, but I don't have enough strong evidence to do anything about it yet. There's still much to investigate. I wonder if he was referring to the two hueveros who had been arrested by the National Police?"

"I don't know. I get the impression that Daniela wouldn't take anything Señor Rodriquez says seriously. My gut instinct is that he's playing to the crowd and the media. I'll make a quick trip to Playa Soledad and get to the hospital as quickly as I can. I'm relieved she's getting medical help." Laura let out a big sigh. "Antonio, thank you for getting her to the hospital. I'm so grateful you were able to check in on her."

"I'm happy I was able to help. We'll see you soon."

Chapter 33

The Santa Fe pulled up and parked where the sand met the road at Playa Soledad. Laura spotted a hatchery volunteer and asked, "How are things going?"

"We've just released 50 eggs. See Tomas and Eva over there?" The volunteer pointed to two people at surfs edge.

Laura smiled as she watched a few hatchlings smaller than the palm of a hand make their way back to the ocean. "Has anything changed with the new security? Are you seeing any new vandalism? I'll need to update Daniela."

"Everything is good. Someone from the Fuerza Publica is at the hatchery around the clock, so no vandalism or threats have been made to the few who have stayed on," the volunteer said. "We're concerned no one is available to watch the rest of the playa and hope we're not missing any new nests. Peak turtle season just passed, so we have that going for us. I think we've saved all the eggs we could this season." Laura nodded and shook his hand. "Thanks to each of you for sticking around after the situation with Gabriel, I know Daniela appreciates the loyalty."

She walked north of the hatchery to the edge of the surf and stared at the vastness of the sea in front of her. The water was cool and refreshing as it lapped over her feet on such a muggy day. Taking in a deep breath of the salty air, she thought about her time in Costa Rica and the friends she'd made. Memories of Gabriel and the garlic fish they shared at El Chevicito had sealed their friendship. She remembered his assistance with her scuba diving lessons. Now Daniela was in the hospital, and Anna and Bianca had left. Laura thought fondly of their trip to Gandoca Manzanillo for zip lining and wondered how they were doing. She'd lost a dear friend and worried Daniela's business could be in jeopardy. She listened to the rhythm of the ocean soothing her sadness.

***

Esteban parked a short distance from Laura, and sat in his sporty Samurai watching her at the hatchery. Then saw his opportunity. The balaclava went over his head, and he grabbed his semiautomatic Glock from the glove box. His approach was quiet. She wasn't paying attention to her surroundings. He grabbed her in a vise-like hold. "Why will you not leave this beach alone? Why did you not go home with the rest of them? You and your friend need to stop with this crusade. We gave you a warning once. I'm not afraid to hurt you," he said into her ear.

Laura got a whiff of a stale, sweaty odor and felt a spray of spittle on her neck. She instinctively reached for his left arm at the elbow, moved herself to his left trying to get her right foot and knee behind his. Bending forward she moved her left foot and felt his body move over hers. His weight became less stable as he tumbled to the ground. Running before becoming fully upright, her feet dug into the loose sand slowing her. He grabbed her left foot as she was moving away and she toppled face first into the sand.

As she tried to turn and right herself, Esteban pulled his gun aiming it at her and kicked her in the solar plexus and lower ribs several times. "This is your last warning; the next time I'll shoot. Leave the country now, you don't belong here."

Laura groaned as she lay there curled in a fetal position. She was sure he had broken some ribs. It hurt to breath. She had to get up, get back to San José. It took her a couple of minutes to sit, she looked around. No one in the area to witness this. She looked up toward her vehicle hoping to spot her assailant. A cherry red car was leaving the area, a small sport SUV with a canvas top, but she couldn't be sure. Was it the guy that assaulted her?

Walking gingerly back to the Santa Fe, holding her ribs and trying not to breathe too deeply, tears of pain welled in her eyes. Grabbing her phone, she was thankful she had a signal.

"Antonio, I've been attacked. I think I have broken ribs."

"What! Where?"

"Playa Soledad. Middle of the day. No witnesses. I was standing along the shoreline, lost in my thoughts. I picked up an odd smell just before..." she paused. "He grabbed me, I broke free, but he caught my leg and that stopped me. He kicked me while I was on the ground."

"Did you see him?"

"No, he was wearing a ski mask. He was taller than me. I could tell from how he held me. Larger and broader and had a deep voice from what I could tell. He was wearing a red t-shirt and long black nylon shorts. Could be overweight but with that sloppy look I couldn't really tell. Dark skin, but that could describe anyone around here."

"Did he say anything?"

"He warned me and Daniela to stop our campaign for beach security. Said they'd hurt us if we didn't stop. He may have been driving one of those red sporty SUV's like a Samurai I think it's called, but I'm not positive. I couldn't see the license number. He must be part of the group that killed Gabriel why else would threaten and injure me? He said he would shoot the next time he saw me."

Antonio could hear the fear and pain in her voice. "Do you need medical attention? Can you make a report to the police while you're there? It would be best to do it in their jurisdiction right away."

"I'll tell the security guy at the hatchery but I don't want it to take too long. It hurts quite a bit. Do you think Daniela will be okay if I stay with the Valverdes tonight? I should get some ice on this. I can see a doctor when I get back. Not much that can be done if the ribs are broken except to limit my movements."

Laura made another report and the security detail called it in. She didn't have much hope that anything would come of it and had more faith in Antonio.

***

Rafael stood at his window watching the San José traffic congestion below, he heard the other side of the line pick up. "Wendigo, I've come upon some information. The OIJ official, Señor De La Torres, has one of your men in the Witness Protection Program. Where, I don't know as that information has suddenly disappeared."

"I thought he was watching over that volunteer that stayed behind. I'll follow up with Esteban." Making note Wendigo continued, "I understand you made a speech in Limón today. One of my men was there. Sounds like you're living up to your promises."

"Have you made additional investments into members of the forensics team?"

"Yes, they'll delay the reporting of information they uncover. I need to know who Mr. De La Torres's superior is."

"You should know that I'm hearing rumors in my office that cell phone numbers have been traced and those suspects will be questioned if they've not already occurred." After searching his database, Rafael finished the conversation by giving Wendigo the name of Antonio's superior.

Just as the call ended with Rafael, Wendigo's phone rang again. "Hola."

"It's Esteban, just came from Playa Soledad. I've extended a threat to that volunteer who didn't leave. She'll be moving a lot slower for a couple of weeks."

"Good. I just spoke with Rafael. Your suspicions were correct about De La Torres. He is the lead of the investigation. Did you know that they have one of your men in the Witness Protection Program? You better find him and kill him before he brings everyone down."

"¡Mierda! I'm placing a bet it's Manuel. He was laying low for a couple of days and now we can't find him. He left his post at the Fuerza Publica. He can talk, but there's no proof, so no arrests. I'm still in the Limón area, I'll personally go knock on his door."

"Two cell phones your men stole have been used since this unfortunate accident and the numbers traced. You might want to find out who the men are and take care of that situation. I'm not happy Esteban. I see that more drugs are being seized in the Caribbean and Drug Enforcement has started to focus on the Pacific traffic as well. We were winning the drug war until your men got out of control," Wendigo lit a cigarillo and continued.

"This additional attention costs us millions of dollars. Your country votes for a new Presidente in a year. That means current officials on our side may not stay in their positions. If we can't deliver the goods on schedule, then we won't affect those elections. Control your men, or I will. You like your status in society? You like being in charge? Then do your damn job and fix this mess, NOW!" After a few more expletives Wendigo cut the call.

Esteban didn't appreciate being spoken to in that manner. He was well aware Wendigo could cut him off, he knew the part he played. He was now incensed by Manuel, by this cell phone debacle. He had some investigating of his own to do.

***

"Hi Maria, it's Laura, is it possible for me to spend the night there?"

"Of course, are you in Limón?"

"Yes, I came to listen to the MINAE speech today. Daniela is ill and is in the hospital. I stopped at Playa Soledad after the speech and was attacked. I think the person is from the group that kidnapped us."

"Oh no! Of course, do you need us to pick you up?"

"No, I have Daniela's car. I'm pretty sore though and really tired. These last couple of weeks have been quite stressful. Do you have an ice pack? I think my ribs are broken."

"Are you sure you don't want me to take you to a doctor?"

"No, that's not necessary. Just ice for now."

"Of course, I'll put an ice pack together right away."

"Thank you. I hate to impose but you were the only person I could think to call."

"How soon can you be here? I'll get the ice pack ready. Are you hungry would you like me to fix you something to eat?"

"No, I just really need a friend right now. I'll be there shortly."

***

At Hospital San Vincente de Paul, Daniela had been sleeping when the nurse came back in to check the wraps and take her temperature, she woke to the nurse's touch. "Hi Daniela, I'm your nurse Maria. Do you know where you are?"

"No, why do I need a nurse?" Daniela surveyed the white walls surrounding her.

"You're at the hospital. Your friend, Antonio, brought you here. You had a very high fever, we were worried about you. How are you feeling?"

"Sleepy." Daniela said in a hoarse whisper.

"Your fever is dropping. That's good news. The damp wraps and the acetaminophen are doing their job. I've put some cream on your rash to help the itching and make you more comfortable."

"Thank you. Why am I here?" she asked again scrunching her eyes in confusion.

"Your friend was worried about you, you were feverish and didn't seem to recognize him." Maria looked over at Antonio with worry. Daniela rolled her head to where the nurse was looking and saw Antonio. Recognition hit.

"Hi, I guess I owe you thanks. Do I have the flu?" she asked Antonio. "Where's Laura?"

"She went to Limón today, in your place. She asked me to stop by and check on you. When I came by, you were very pale and looked weak. I took your pulse and you were slurring words, so I brought you here. I called Laura while you slept." Antonio reassured her.

"Shouldn't you be doing an investigation and making arrests?" asked Daniela.

"Sounds like you're feeling better," Antonio's voice was tinged with humor. "I'm waiting on some information I've requested. I'd taken a break when I went to the condo to check on you."

The doctor entered interrupting the exchange. "I see our patient is awake. Hi, my name is Doctor Castillo. I understand the nurse has given you some information and I'm happy to see that your fever is starting to break. The illness you have is serious and it is good you are here."

"This isn't just a bad flu?"

"Ms. Segura you have contracted dengue fever."

Daniela's eyes grew larger as her mouth fell open.

"This is an illness caused by multiple mosquito bites specifically from the *Aedes aegypti* mosquito. It tends to mimic influenza but the measles type rash, and the bright red palms that you have help us to diagnose this. Unfortunately, due to the extra rain we've received, the illness made its way into the San José area. It's been quite prevalent in many hospitals recently."

"What do I need to do to stop this?"

"There is not much we can do. It needs to run its course. We'll keep you comfortable while you're here by continuing the acetaminophen and the IV to rehydrate you. It is very important you stay under medical supervision while we give you the medication to avoid any complications that might arise. We're preparing a room for you, you'll need stay overnight. Possibly a couple of days. It can take up to six weeks to recover."

"Six weeks. That's not possible, I have too much to do," she cried out trying to sit up.

"Every person can react and recover differently, but this illness has put serious stress on your system. You'll feel very weak and tired for a good stretch of time. We need to watch you, the fever, and the rash to make sure everything clears as it should. Now I need you to relax and get some more rest."

"I'll stay right here until they get you into a room." Antonio reassured her as he pulled a chair up to her bed. "Laura will be back tomorrow. She's spending the evening with Clemente and Maria." He didn't want to let on about Laura's attack and wanted Daniela to focus on getting better.

Chapter 34

Antonio left the emergency room and dialed his office for an update. They relayed additional information related to rubber from the inflatable. They'd determined a similarity to those used in local river rafting outfitters and were in the process of compiling a list of tour operators and their business owners for questioning. Antonio also requested employee rosters.

No sooner did he finish that call when another rang. He recognized Laura's number.

"I made the report, I'm now with Maria, how's Daniela? Can I speak with her?"

He relayed the treatment and diagnosis adding, "I think Daniela was in shock when the doctor said it would take six weeks for recovery."

"Dengue fever. Oh my god, what does that mean?"

Antonio explained it further, extinguishing some of Laura's fear.

"Did you have a chance to ask her about the laptop and the patio door?"

"No, we've barely spoken. She just started to recognize her surroundings. I'll ask her in the morning. They should have a room ready for her soon."

"Anything new on the investigation today?"

"Not much. I spoke with two persons of interest regarding their whereabouts but the information they provided doesn't coincide with the night of the kidnapping. They mentioned viewing a fútbol game on the night in question, but it contradicts other dates they gave me. If they were watching this game, it would have ended, and they'd still have time to be at the playa when the event occurred. I'll consider them suspects in the kidnapping, theft of the cell phones, and hope to tag on a tampering with an active investigation for what appears to be falsifying information. Just need to clear the arrest warrant. I do have one confidential witness, but need to corroborate that information with evidence. I don't have all those pieces yet."

"That sounds like a lot of progress." Laura was heartened.

"Maybe. The forensics team is involved too, could take another week to get what I need. There won't be an arrest by the 18th, so I don't know what the Minister of Environment was talking about at the rally you were at." Antonio located a vending machine and reached in his pocket for change, "How are you feeling? Will you be back tomorrow?"

"I'll be fine. Yes, I'm coming back tomorrow, I just want you to get those bastards."

***

Antonio headed back to his place after deciding he would need a security guard for Laura and Daniela once she was out of the hospital. It would take a couple of days to convince his supervisor to take on the expense of an armed security guard for the women until arrests could be made in the Montenegro case. Tonight was Saturday. Tomorrow was church with his mother, and anyone working the case would be off. No action until Monday frustrated him.

He grabbed a cold cerveza from the fridge, stuck a frozen dinner in the microwave and opened his laptop. Working at his kitchen table, he Googled the names of the suspects that Manuel Jimenez gave him. He confirmed via Facebook that Pedro Villalobos Tres was the same man he spoke with. No indication of self-incrimination on his page as it didn't look often used. He checked Alonso Mendes Morales, but nothing came up. Then Luis Rodrigues Salas. BINGO.

Here was a picture of a skinny kid with dark wavy hair holding an AK-47, bare chested, in a plaid pair of pajama pants, and an S-shaped tattoo on his left fore arm. The cover picture. Unbelievable. Luis bragged to the world that he possessed an assault type weapon, *well, well, well. Now that I know what you look like Mr. Rodrigues Salas, I'm coming for you.* He knew he could bring

Pedro up on theft and kidnapping charges and probably charge Alonso with being an accomplice and supplying false information.

He wanted to track down Luis and get him on stalking charges and carrying an un-registered weapon. He hoped his fingerprints were on the AK-47 found in Pocora then get him on kidnapping charges too. He was confident he could make three arrests. He continued looking for Esteban Rojas Madrigal. Not much on a profile, but the name did come up as manager of one of the Pacuare tour outfits, Pacuare Rafting Adventures. Antonio was getting excited now. Monday morning, he would request the business license for this outfitter.

***

Maria had prepared the room Laura used previously and added some extra pillows to help prop her up. She helped Laura to the bed and gave her the ice pack.

"What happened?"

Laura recited the events again. "I can't believe it happened again on the same beach, in the middle of the day, sunlight and everything. How did anyone even know I would be there?" Laura asked.

"Maybe they were expecting Daniela, she would've been the one who would normally check in on the hatchery," Maria replied.

"True. If it's the group she suspected, they did have people watching the beach, at least according to Gabriel." Laura winched when she took a breath, "How is it possible that I could be attacked on the same beach twice? Now I'm really ticked off. At least I was able to defend myself this time. I didn't know he had a gun, he could have shot me." Her heart raced, and her breaths felt like a vice squeezing her side.

"He didn't. Focus on that."

"I'll be honest, Maria. I was hoping to make a permanent move to Costa Rica. After this, I'm ready to go home. What the hell was I thinking anyway? I don't agree with every law back home, but I sure feel more protected. At least the illusion of protection is stronger. I'll stay until Antonio can make arrests and Daniela is back and ready to fight again."

"Antonio? You're on a first name basis with the OIJ guy?"

"Yeah, he's been very helpful and… friendly. He gave me his phone number and it's easier to call him when we need something. He doesn't seem to mind."

"He sure is handsome. Now layback and get some rest, Clemente should be home soon. Do you feel like eating anything at all?"

"Maybe just some soup if that's not a problem. I need to focus on breathing, I can't let this slow me down. I need to help until Daniela can get better."

***

Esteban was furious. He thought he'd taken care of issues and given stern warnings to the men about their mistakes. Now Manuel was gone. Which of his men were stupid enough to use the cell phones? He headed to Manuel's home, and hoped to grab the wife. The house was closed—no one home. He broke in. Although furniture and the kitchen were intact, belongings were missing from the bedroom. Damn, the OIJ got there first. Esteban spoke with a couple of neighbors but they hadn't seen anyone in a couple of days. They did say they saw vehicles leave in the evening a day or so ago. He put his focus back on the phones; guessed it could be Luis, Pedro, or Alonso. It wouldn't have been Beni. He was busy with the boats and Esteban trusted him. He would question the others.

***

"*¿Mi querida amiga*, how are you?" asked Clemente as he gently hugged Laura.

"I'll be fine. Clemente, when I was staying here last, we never really talked about what you did for a living. Señor De La Torres asked me when he questioned me and I didn't have an answer."

"Ah, yes we spoke mostly of Limón and the *tortugas*."

"So what do you do? You work at the ports, right?

"Sí. I'm a manager there. My company, we help repair the machinery on the banana ships that come in, or provide parts they may need."

"And how is business?" Laura carefully tried adjusting a pillow behind her.

Seeing her struggle Clemente helped her. "Well... things are slowing down a bit. There's been talk of expansion in Moin. A port there that could affect ours. We've had to let many men go. The only other jobs in the area are tourist services or, unfortunately, activities that aren't legal."

"Like drugs?" Laura looked up at him.

"Yes, and the poaching you've witnessed. Also theft, so many undesirable choices in this part of the country."

"But your job is ok, right?"

"For now. That is why we also help LSTC when we can, it is additional income for us."

"Did Antonio question you and Maria too? I mean, after the kidnappings?"

"Sí. He wanted to know our backgrounds and our relationship with LSTC. I'm sure it's just routine, nothing to worry about. We have nothing to hide."

Chapter 35

In his Sunday best, a pressed pair of black trousers and a stark white short-sleeve *guayabera*, Antonio blended in with the crowd at his mother's church that morning. He met up with Laura at the hospital following the service.

"Hi, you look nice, just come from church?" Laura said taking note of his caramel skin playing against the white of his shirt. He didn't look intimidating to her anymore.

"Sí, I take my mother every Sunday. Then we have lunch together. I told her I was going to stop by and check on things here first. How are you feeling today?"

"Sore, it hurts to take too deep a breath, but the ice packs Maria gave me helped." She kept her left arm folded over her abdomen.

"Let's have a nurse take a look at you before I take you to Daniela's room."

He introduced her to the nurse, confirmed she had broken ribs and the best thing she could do was the ice. The nurse encouraged Laura to breathe deeply to avoid pneumonia.

Antonio and Laura walked slowly to Daniela's room.

"You're starting to look much more like yourself. You gave me a scare yesterday." Antonio told Daniela. Everyone exchanged pleasantries. Now that Daniela was alert, Laura filled her in on the hatchlings and her rib issue.

"I noticed the terrace door was opened when I came over to check on you yesterday, had you gotten up to open it, or work on the laptop?" Antonio asked.

"I don't think so. I don't remember getting up from the bed. Why?"

"Just wondering," Antonio didn't want to make her anxious.

"I did have a dream that struck me as odd," Daniela said, "Someone was sitting on me, a man, tall and thin wearing a blue shirt. I tried to fight, to scream but couldn't make a sound. I blinked and he was gone."

"Maybe its just your mind unwrapping itself from the fever," suggested Laura.

"Maybe," Daniela said.

Antonio made a mental note to check the condo for possible fingerprints. Could it be related? Was it just a dream? Given the additional assault on Laura he wouldn't rule either possibility out.

"How's the investigation coming?" Daniela asked.

"I plan to visit a river rafting outfitter tomorrow in Siquirres." Antonio rearranged things on the bedside table. Laura wondered if he was neat or nervous.

"Oh, have you got a lead?"

"Yes, we have someone in the Witness Protection Program who named several people. One includes a manager of a tour company. I spent last night searching the names online and found some interesting information. The forensic team is analyzing some new evidence. Hopefully we'll have something more concrete within a week or two. I need to be able to tie evidence to these individuals to make arrests."

"That would be wonderful." Laura said.

"It's a good thing you two are roommates. I'm getting security for you. Laura can assist in your recovery and with MINAE business, and I can keep you both safe in one place." Antonio's expression darkened. "Daniela, I think the assault on Laura was meant for you."

***

Antonio burst with anticipation early Monday morning as he raced to his office to gather the employee list for Pacuare Rafting Adventures. His gut told him Esteban Rojas Madrigal was the person he needed to speak with. He had a hunch the employee list would include Luis Rodriquez Salas, Pedro Villalobos Tres and Alonso Mendez Morales. He wanted to see names in print to be sure.

After a brief argument with his superior over assigning an officer to guard Daniela's condo, Antonio secured one. The officer, in cooperation with the Publica Fuerza in Heredia, would start once Daniela was released from the hospital. The agreement included Antonio being the chaperone should one or both of them need to leave the condo, providing that task worked into his investigation schedule.

The list of rafting outfitters that served the Pacuare River was delivered while he was with his superior. He glanced through the employee list and spotted the names, giving him written confirmation. The business license was legitimate. He just needed to connect the forensic evidence to them. He looked forward to paying Pacuare Rafting Adventures a visit and formulated ideas for multiple arrests.

Chapter 36

A cherry red Samurai was parked in the empty lot of Pacuare Rafting Adventures. Esteban had called Luis, Pedro and Alonso into the office to prep for an upcoming group and he needed to find out about the cell phones.

Luis arrived first, his right hand still bandaged from losing his fingers. "Luis, the night of that unfortunate death you caused, do you remember who took care of the cell phones that I ordered be taken?" Esteban asked.

"I was with you when you hit that biologist on the back of the head. I didn't see what the others were doing. Pedro, Alonso, and Manuel would've been available to take the belongings from them. Why do you ask?"

"I was looking for personal affects in the warehouse where you and Beni dropped off the equipment the night of your accident. It looks like we're missing two phones. You wouldn't have taken one would you?"

"No. Beni had to do the delivery himself. He brought me to a clinic. I was out once I got pain meds. Maybe he took them."

"Perhaps you're right. I need you to get the locker areas cleaned out, check that there are locks and keys on each, and empty the trash. We have a large group coming tomorrow and we need to prepare."

"Sí señor, I'll get right on that," Luis had a renewed respect for authority after losing a few digits.

Pedro and Alonso arrived together, as always. "*Buenos dias jefe*. What do you need us to do today?" Pedro asked.

"We have a large group coming tomorrow. Luis has started working on the locker areas. I need you to do an inventory of the food supplies and beverages in the terrace café and vending machines. Make sure we have plenty of napkins, glasses, and other supplies. Twenty people are expected. I want everything ready this afternoon. Alonso, I need you to make sure the digital camera equipment is clean and in working order, that we have enough DVD's for purchase in the photo shop, and make sure the t-shirts, postcards, and stuffed animals are replenished in the gift shop."

"What about my post at the condo?" Alonso asked.

"One day won't make a difference. That Segura bitch is in the hospital, and that volunteer is in a world of hurt."

Alonso shrugged. "OK."

Esteban wrinkled his forehead in curiosity "One more thing, we seem to be missing two cell phones from the inventory I reviewed in the warehouse. Do either of you happen to know anything about that?"

Pedro and Alonso glanced at each other. "No, not a thing. We put them in a sack with the flashlights, shoes, and jewelry we took. It should all be together." Pedro replied a little too quickly Esteban thought.

"Well then, I guess I'll need to check with Manuel and Beni."

The two men rushed off to their tasks.

Esteban was not satisfied with his answer. He would find another way to pry the truth from Pedro.

***

Finally, a sunny day in June, the rain had let up. Antonio was in a good mood, looking forward to his visit to Pacuare River Adventures.

He pulled into the parking area and saw a cherry red, canvassed topped, sporty vehicle and thought back to Laura's description of the vehicle she saw drive away the day she was attacked. His heart sped up in anticipation. Everything was coming together. He took the main walkway toward the office and glimpsed a bank of lockers to his left. A skinny kid with dark wavy hair wore a large bandage on his right hand, and was cleaning the area. He moved to get a closer look.

"Excuse me, can you tell me where the main office is?" Antonio asked.

"It's right over there," Luis pointed with his left hand, bringing the S-shaped dragon tattoo into view.

"Nice work you have there," Antonio commented "Does your tattoo have any particular significance?"

"No," responded Luis, "I loved the design. Looks tough, right?"

"It certainly does. Well thank you for the directions." Antonio walked by a garden area, a terrace café, restrooms, the gift shop, photo area, and found the general office. He stepped inside and saw a man in his mid-forties with greasy looking shoulder length hair, belly paunch, and a plump, small-featured face sitting at a desk. "How can I help you?" the man asked in a throaty voice. The deep sound didn't match the childish face.

Antonio introduced himself as an OIJ officer, "I'm here to get some information regarding white water rafting."

Esteban recognized the OIJ insignia on Antonio's shirt. "I'm Esteban, the manager here. Is this official business or are you looking to book a tour for yourself?"

"It's not official. I'm just trying to gather some general information I was hoping you might be able to help. I want to know specifically about tours on the Pacuare River, and your company sounds like a great place to start."

"Well then, I'll do my best to answer your questions. Please have a seat," Esteban said agreeably as he moved his arm toward the chair opposite him.

"Let's start with how tours usually get booked. Do you book them yourselves or do you go through some of the agencies in the area?" Antonio asked.

"We do both. There are several reputable adventure tour companies throughout Costa Rica. Many of the main offices are out of San José, but we also work with the groups out of the Arenal and Limón areas. We have packages they sell. Could be anything from one to multiple days."

"What would a one-day tour look like? How many people take part in a typical tour?"

"Group size can depend, anything from a small group of four up to 20. We have different size rafts to accommodate the group. The larger the group the more rafts we use. A typical raft holds six to eight people comfortably with the rough water in the rapids. The one-day trip averages eighteen miles, taking a full day to hit all 52 rapids." Esteban opened a brochure and placed it in front of Antonio.

"The first four miles are class II and III. About 40 minutes into the river we hit Pacuare River Gorge which is reputed to have five miles of some of the best white water in Costa Rica and recently rated as the fifth best in the world. These rapids can be classed as level IV and V, and have names like Terciopelo Snake, Double Drop, and Pin Ball. We take the tour past the Huacas Waterfall that has a 150-foot drop, then the river opens up to a stretch of about five miles." Esteban's fingers traced the map on the brochure as he continued his memorized sales pitch.

"This allows an opportunity to rest, some like to float in the river in this area," he pointed to a picture. "It's a chance to spot wildlife, look at the rainforests and then there are four more rapids before finishing here at the base. We have showers, lockers, food, so you can relax after such an adrenaline raising adventure."

"How do people get to the river, do they start here, or do tour vans pick them up?" Antonio asked.

"Tour busses from the outfitters we've contracted with will pick them up. The first drop is here, so they can put belongings in the lockers. Then we issue them their life jackets, helmet and paddle. We go through a safety briefing and then they get back on the bus to bring them where the rafts are waiting. Just depends on how long of a trip they will be doing."

"Are the vans the typical olive green tourist buses that you see throughout the country?"

"Usually, again it depends on the size of the group. The black shuttle buses are used when it's a smaller group."

"What type of rafts are used for these excursions?" Antonio was making notes.

"We use a commercial rated inflatable raft with an air floor for flexibility needed in the rapids. They're made of a heavy-duty rubber coated fabric that can handle the extreme use they get."

"Is there a typical manufacturer used for this purpose?"

"There are several different manufacturers, you've probably heard of Zodiac brand, there is also Saturn, Vanguard, and we use Sotar Elite. Again, the type of raft used depends on the use and the number of people."

"Are these rafts typically grey and black?" Antonio was thinking of the samples found.

"They can be. They also come in blues, yellows, reds. I know some of our competitors will use only yellow or only blue. It helps to tell the competitors apart, and there's a discount when you buy in bulk."

"What color rafts do you use?"

"It varies, depending on the size of the raft, and the length of the trip. We typically use the grey/black for the longer trips, blue for the smaller rafts. Ordering replacements, we may order another color just because it helps give us a visual on what the newest inventory is."

"Could these rafts be used in the ocean or are they just for river rafting?" Antonio glanced at his notes again.

Esteban paused and sat straighter in his chair. The only sound was a hum from the oscillating fan sitting atop a filing cabinet.

"They can be used for ocean travel. Typically, inflatable boats used for ocean excursions are of the same grade but have rigid floor boards to give it a sturdier ride moving through the waves."

"I would assume that your peak business is done during dry seasons when the tourists are here, correct?"

"For the most part. The water is actually a little lower then, but as you say, the tourists are here. Water levels in the rainy season make a more exciting ride."

"What kind of staff does a river outfitter need for these adventures?"

"Depends. Are multiple groups going out the same day? Then we need someone to staff the café, clean the restrooms, work the gift shop. There are usually two crew men per raft. On a slow day we would be looking at a minimum of eight employees." Esteban looked at his schedule, "Let me give you an example. Tomorrow, we have a group of twenty scheduled, so I'll need eight men to man four boats, and another four to cover base business. I keep a group of fifteen on payroll through peak season, and a minimum of eight throughout the year, but others are on call."

"Thank you for your time. You've answered my questions." Antonio stood to leave.

Esteban reached for a card on his desk, "Here is my business card, let me know if I can be of further assistance. You should consider taking a trip yourself, you'd find it quite exhilarating."

"I'll keep that in mind." Antonio offered his hand, then carefully picked up the brochure.

Antonio returned to his truck. His mind was working overtime. *I have an ID on the possible leader, Luis, Pedro, and Alonso. There has to be at least one more. I sure hope the evidence and DNA link them to the kidnappings and murder.*

Esteban closed the door behind Antonio and was immediately suspicious of the questions. *It's Manuel, what has he told them?* He wasted no time in contacting Wendigo. "I have the identity of Señor De La Torres. He just came to see me. Have you paid the forensics team to lose evidence?" Esteban asked.

"Yes, a couple of techs inside the forensic department are delaying processes and reporting technical difficulties with equipment." Wendigo said.

"Should I have someone rough him up? Put a tail on him?" Esteban pulled out his pocket-size book of contacts.

"That'll be fine."

"By the way, Alonso said the Segura woman's in the hospital."

Wendigo, in his plush leather desk chair, swiveled to look out at the high rises surrounding his office and downtown Baranquilla, Colombia. "Good. Rafael is keeping his ears close to the investigation also. It appears OIJ has a theory but no hard evidence." He paused to take a sip of scotch. "You should know, Pedro's name came up with one of the stolen cell phones they traced."

"Interesting, I had my suspicions. I'll have to teach him a lesson." Esteban said.

Chapter 37

Antonio gained a surge of energy from this recent information. Seeing a couple of his suspects gave him confidence he was closing in. *Time to tread carefully. This information is still circumstantial.* He headed back to the forensics lab to follow up on background results, the investigation at Pocora and the fingerprints on the AK-47. He put in a call to his supervisor and shared an idea he had for making multiple arrests simultaneously. Timing was crucial for success.

He reached Laura, let her know things were moving in a positive direction, and asked about Daniela.

"That's great news. Daniela's doing much better today. She said she still has body aches, but they're getting her up to walk several times a day. The rash is fading and her headaches are gone. She's much more sociable than she's been. They'll keep her over one more night and are saying she can probably leave tomorrow. You'll want to be sure that security guard is in place. Can you join me when we get her checked out? I might need help getting her up the stairs." Laura hoped to see him again.

"Happy to hear she's feeling better. Depending on time of release tomorrow, I might be able to help. I'll have to let you know tomorrow. I'm sure you're both anxious to get back to normal." Antonio responded with a blush he was thankful no one could see. He just had to figure out how to spend more time alone with Laura.

***

Esteban drove to Estrada while smoking a Vegas de Santiago "Puro" cigar. *If I can't get the truth out of Pedro, perhaps persuading his girlfriend will do the trick.* He watched Susanna hanging clothes on the line. He pulled to the side of the road, put the sporty vehicle in park, and took his Glock handgun from the glove box along with the balaclava.

Around the house he grabbed her from behind, slamming a hand over her mouth. He pulled her back towards him and put the gun's cold muzzle to her neck.

"Shhhh, no screaming," Esteban whispered into her ear. "Your boyfriend has been lying to me. You need to call him and tell him to come home right away. Do you understand?"

She nodded, a tear drop slid down her cheek. Esteban pulled her inside the house, sat her down on a kitchen chair, and pulled a couple of plastic tie straps from his pocket to secure her to it.

"I'm calling him now. When I hold the phone to you, tell him that you're in trouble and to come alone. Do not tell him anything more, or you will be hurt. Do you understand?"

She nodded.

When Pedro answered, he moved the phone next to her ear. She followed instructions. They would now wait for him to arrive. Esteban sat across from her, rested his cigar on the edge of the table where its offensive smell floated into the air, and pointed his gun at her forehead.

***

"*Mi querida, Mi querida,*" Pedro ran into the house screaming, "*¿Que esta mal?*" He froze when he saw a man with the balaclava and gun pointed at Susanna. "What is going on?" he asked.

"You lied to me Pedro. About the cell phone, you lied didn't you?"

"No, No, I swear." Pedro realized Esteban was behind the mask.

"Pedro, remember when we had the conversation about the missing cell phones?"

"Yes, I told you I didn't know anything about that."

"Don't make me hurt your *bella compañera*. You know I will," Esteban pulled back the slide on his Glock. "You and Alonso were in charge of getting the phones and belongings, no one else touched them. Now what have you done with the phones?" His voice raised in anger.

"Please, please, don't hurt her. I swear I don't have them," he pleaded.

"Here's what doesn't make sense to me. I've been told your name has come up in the OIJ investigation on a cell phone number trace. Seems to me you've had one of those cell phones in your possession. As a matter of fact, THIS PHONE IS IN POLICE HANDS." Esteban turned the gun toward Pedro.

"Ok, ok. I'll tell you the truth. I gave the phone to my girlfriend as a birthday present. I thought I had wiped everything clean. I didn't think it could be traced."

"You didn't think is the point. What should your punishment be for not thinking?" Esteban took a fresh drag off the cigar.

Pedro was starting to perspire, his pupils grew larger, his nervousness increased with the close proximity of Esteban. Esteban removed the cigar from his mouth, took a look at the lighted end and put it back in his mouth. He reached out and grabbed Pedro by the throat with his free hand. Esteban, with the cigar still in his mouth, moved his head just enough to burn Pedro's right cheek with the cigar. The stench of burning flesh sat heavy in the room. Pedro tried to grab his arms and move them away as he screamed, but Esteban moved the barrel of the gun to his neck.

"There. Now you will see your mistake every day you see yourself. It's to remind you that you don't have power to make such decisions. You've made a serious error. Perhaps, the point would become clearer were I to scar your *compañera* too."

"No! No, please stop," Pedro pled as he dropped to his knees and broke into tears.

"Pedro, you have put our operation in great jeopardy. You're lucky you've not been arrested for kidnapping. This is my last warning. Any word to the policía from you or her about this and someone will end up dead."

"Yes, Yes, of course. Please let her go."

Esteban put the gun away, turned and walked out, slamming the door behind him.

***

Alone again at the condo, Laura had more time to replay the kidnapping, and her time with Gabriel and the other women. Memories of the mess that had been her marriage, her ex-husband's verbal abuse, his lack of financial support, and the constant tenseness of her body from incessant work demands came back to her. She'd enjoyed her first four weeks in this country, and finally relaxed. Until the incident on the beach with the gun, she hadn't really felt threatened. She'd naively chalked it up to being at the wrong place at the wrong time, grateful she hadn't been raped. Logic had taken over. *It could have been so much worse.* She thought about Gabriel and the zip-lining, the night they all went dancing. Pure simple fun. Happiness. Peacefulness. She needed to hold onto those positive thoughts and continue to help Daniela with her campaign. The idea of becoming a conservation advocate back home interested her. Thinking of a change in career gave her hope.

***

Antonio made a quick stop by the hospital on his way back into San José.

"Remember that dream you told me about, the man that was sitting on you?"

"Yes,"

"Well, I think someone may have broken into the condo while you were asleep, I'm going to meet Laura over there tonight to check for fingerprints."

"Do you think this is related to what happened to Gabriel?"

"I do. The security guard will arrive shortly after we get you back home tomorrow. I'll give him a call and walk the area with him once your home."

"Great, I'm looking forward to it. I hate to cut our conversation short, but I'm really tired again. I hope you don't mind."

"Not at all, your health is the priority right now. Laura will give me a call tomorrow after she speaks with your doctor. I'll say goodnight." Antonio turned to leave.

"Thanks for the visit, good night."

Chapter 38

At the condo, Laura greeted Antonio and the forensic technician at the door.

"Have you touched anything since you've been here?" Antonio asked.

"No, I just got here a few minutes ago. I've only opened the front door and put my purse on the kitchen island."

"Good. We'll start with the patio door since I know that was opened. Is the laptop here? That was opened, we need to check that. I suspect we'll find at least two sets of prints; yours and Daniela's." Antonio led the technician to the patio door and pointed to the laptop on the kitchen island.

"Let me get your fingerprints so we have something to compare and eliminate." Antonio placed a small kit on the island. "I saw Daniela today. She's eager to come home."

"I bet she is. I'm planning on making her a welcome home dinner of *arroz con pollo*. Will you be able to join us? You've been so helpful, and I'd like to repay you in some small way."

"I'd enjoy that. I'm sorry your vacation didn't turn out the way you hoped it would."

"For the most part, it did. The kidnapping and being on the wrong beach could have happened to me in California if I'm honest with myself. We have those same problems in the States. I look at it as a matter of circumstance. I came here to get a better perspective on my life. And, that was granted." Laura hoped the optimism she was trying to convince herself of, was working on him.

"I'm happy you have a positive attitude about it. I'd hate to have you dislike my beautiful country. It's so much more than what happened to you and your friends, but your experience contradicts that." Antonio's faced slacked into sadness.

"Your country is beautiful on so many levels. The people I've met have been generous, but, as with anywhere else in the world, there are unseemly ones too." Laura rolled the ink covered finger tips of her right hand on a card with Antonio's hand guiding hers. She got a fluttery feeling in her stomach when he touched her.

"Can I bring anything for the dinner?" He finished with her prints and started to clean up his supplies.

"Just bring whatever you want to drink. I know Daniela is a big water and fruit juice fan and probably shouldn't have any alcohol while she's recovering. I could use a couple of cervezas myself, could you bring some?" Laura scrubbed her hands in the sink.

"Sure, but I'd like to set some ground rules for tomorrow's dinner," Antonio said.

Laura turned her head over her shoulder and looked at him with concern.

"Can we all get to know each other outside of all this investigative stuff? I'll be spending a lot of time with you and it would be nice to learn more about you and Daniela. What your interests are outside of the MINAE campaign for example, that kind of thing."

"I suppose we could try." Laura dried her hands, turned and looked into his eyes relieved his questions were personal. She hoped she wasn't blushing. "I haven't really had a chance to get to know Daniela on a personal level either. Everything's been about the conservancy and Gabriel, so professional. If we're going to be roomies we need to be able relax around each other a bit."

The technician interrupted their conversation, "It looks like there are smudges on the patio door. I think I was able to get a couple of clean prints. I also took a couple from the lap top. Anything else you'd like me to check?"

"What about the front door? Do you think he jimmied the lock or used the key?" asked Laura.

"The key was where you said it would be when I got here. Were you able to find a different set of prints on the door?" Antonio asked the technician.

"Only smudges. Doesn't appear he broke in. The door jamb wasn't disturbed. Let me check the lock," the technician responded.

"Laura, did you notice anything unusual in the area when you were driving up? Any new cars, bikes, people you don't recognize?" Antonio asked.

"Not really. Everything here is new to me. I haven't been here long enough to notice any patterns. Now that I have a new perspective, I'll keep my eyes open at all times." Laura started twirling her hair, "Will it be ok for us to use the terrace? It's a nice place to have coffee, and Daniela is probably feeling a little closed in at that the hospital."

"Yeah, it should be fine. Keep your eyes open for anything different, like cars driving by, or strange people. The guard will be down below, I'll give you his cell number when I know who the officer will be and you can contact him when necessary. He'll walk the perimeter of the building on a regular basis," Antonio said.

***

Back at his post, Alonso had followed Laura to the hospital and was watching the exit doors. He watched as Antonio, Laura, and a nurse wheeled Daniela out to her SUV. He let Esteban know the pair were on their way back with the officer in tow.

"Just learned from Wendigo there'll be a guard stationed at the condo. You'll need to find another way of monitoring so you don't draw attention to yourself or the car your using," Esteban said.

"I've seen signs for a couple of rooms for rent in the area. I'll take a closer look at those. I'll figure something out." Alonso replied.

***

The three amigos walked up to Daniela's condo together. The sun was shining, a mild breeze blowing from the west. "Wow, what a walk. It feels so good to be outside but I'm tired again. This fatigue is ridiculous," Daniela said as they entered the condo.

"It's good to have you back, just take it easy, I'm here to help." Laura pulled a bar stool to her.

"By the way, now that we're sharing the condo, I hate to kick you out of the bed, but-" Daniela started to say.

"Of course, this is your home. I picked up some extra linens from Price Savers. I'll sleep on the sofa. My ribs feel better when I sleep more upright anyway. Your healing is more important right now."

"Antonio, I hope you'll be making arrests soon so we don't have to be stepping over each other for too long," Daniela said.

Antonio ignored the comment and changed the topic, "I brought a six pack of Imperial, let me put it in the refrigerator. Ignacio will be the guard from Heredia Station watching over you two. He should be here within the hour." He turned to look at Laura, "How soon were you planning on making dinner? I need to swing back to the office and follow up on a few things once Ignacio is here."

"I was thinking of starting it about three, and we'll eat about four. Will that work for you?" Laura asked.

"It should. A few items I need information on seem to be taking too long and I need to keep pushing for results."

"I find it ironic that Ignacio is the name of our security guard. That's Gabriel's father's name. This has to be a good sign." Daniela turned to Laura, "Is there still a MINAE meeting next Tuesday? Are you planning on attending? I'm not sure that I'll be up to it."

"Yes. I saw it on your calendar in the laptop and already planned on being there. Maybe you'll feel a little stronger by then. I'm ready to confront Señor Rodriguez if I have to." Laura looked back to Antonio, "The meeting will be at 2 in the afternoon, will you be able to take me and join the meeting?"

"I'll add it to my calendar. I don't foresee a problem now, but it is a week away anything can happen," he responded.

"Daniela, you should know that Señor Rodriguez mentioned OIJ would have arrests next week. The conservation community is planning a protest march from MINAE to the OIJ building after the Tuesday meeting. I'll attend that too. I spoke to that conservationist from the states that added to your reward the night of Gabriel's vigil. He sought me out when he heard you were in the hospital." Laura moved about the kitchen looking for spices. "Antonio, I realize you're doing your best, but it's important to keep Gabriel's memory alive with the media and keep them focused on the government's need for change."

"You've learned well Laura. Looks like you didn't miss a beat while I was unavailable," Daniela was proud of her student.

Antonio spoke up,"I understand the importance of the march. I'll add to my schedule and walk with you."

"Daniela, I hope you'll be feeling up to it," Laura said. "I know the community will be relieved to see you again."

"Now that, I wouldn't miss for the world. It will give me a goal to focus on," Daniela replied.

There was a knock on the door and Ignacio, the security guard, had arrived. Laura was watching Antonio as he spoke, but thinking *God, Antonio's gorgeous, I'd love to see him without a shirt.*

The men left to walk the building together. All was well for now.

Chapter 39

At the forensics lab, Antonio spoke with the lab techs one of whom said, "The fingerprints for the AK-47 came back, but there's no match in our database. Whoever touched it doesn't have a previous arrest record. Also, a couple of hair strands were found on the victim's clothes. The medical examiner's office sent them over. We're still waiting on DNA results for that, we expect it next week."

Antonio was certain the assault rifle belonged to one of the men involved in the kidnapping. "Will you also check for fingerprints on the cell phone? I'm interested to see if there is a match between that and the AK-47." He hoped it would be Pedro's fingerprints on both.

The second lab tech spoke, "We've determined that the residue found on the bags from the Pocora location was baking soda. We also found traces of cocaine powder on the floor next to those bags, so we've concluded the baking soda was used to cut powdered cocaine at that location."

Antonio had the confirmation he needed about the ranch. It made sense that the helicopter pads would be used for moving the product. The next step was proving that the DNA sample found there could be tied to one of the men involved with the kidnapping. At this point it looked like two separate incidents and that was frustrating to Antonio. He still only had Manuel's confession to tie these two cases together. He wanted arrests soon but had a bad feeling. The delays and excuses given to him by the forensics team nagged him. Something told him that another source might be involved.

The name Wendigo crept into Antonio's thoughts. How much money did this character have and how far did his tentacles reach? He'd sent a message to his supervisor mentioning his concerns and hoped for a meeting with him very soon. He thought he could trust his supervisor, but if drug money was involved there was no telling how high the pay offs went. He suspected that a member of the forensics team was involved. Was it possible that the information they'd found was also being leaked outside the OIJ? He had to figure out how and by who and stop it.

It took a couple of hours for him to go between forensics and his office before he could update the investigation notes. He glanced at the clock on the laptop, after 4, he was late for dinner. He called Laura to apologize and to tell her he was on his way.

***

"**I**'m sorry I'm late, but an investigation takes priority," Antonio said when Laura answered the door.

"We understand. I've kept dinner warm. Are you ready for a cerveza?" Laura asked as she headed to the fridge. "I have some exciting news to share with you. A new development occurred while you were away."

"Okay," he said.

"I received an email from *Rainforest Radio*. They'd learned I was still in town and wanted to interview me regarding the turtles and the kidnapping. They want my perspective. They are also pro-conservation with turtles and thought this would be a great way to educate the public and help increase Tico pressure on the government."

"That is exciting."

"I need to let the public know what a great person Gabriel was, how important the leatherback turtle conservation is and I just happen to be a part of a really important story. Because I'm from the U.S., they said the reach of this radio station could be broadcast on a sister station in Los Angeles. So not only would Ticos hear it, but U.S. citizens could be made aware as well. What a great way to keep the story moving forward. They will post a recording of the interview on their Facebook page, which means I can also share it on my network."

"That's great. When's the interview?"

"On Monday. Will you be able to drive me? They told me to be there at noon, so maybe you could use your lunch break?" Laura's voice surged with energy and excitement as she looked at Antonio like a child begging for a treat.

Antonio took the cold beer offered by Laura. "I'm sure that will be fine. It's great to see you excited about this. It's been a long week for both of you."

"It's hard to believe that it's been a week since Gabriel's funeral, and then that horrible fever and headache started. I'm excited to see that the media and the other conservation agencies have kept pushing this story and supporting LSTC while I've been out of commission," Daniela said. "Laura has done a great job stepping in on short notice." She raised her glass to Laura.

"Dinner is served, come have a seat up here at the bar. Daniela, can I get you a refill?" asked Laura.

"Thank you. I'm afraid I'll just be sticking with water, no cerveza for me." Daniela made a mock pouty face.

They had a wonderful dinner, lots of chit chat and finally a break from talking about Gabriel's death, the investigation, and Daniela's illness. Antonio and Daniela learned a little more about Laura and why her sabbatical was so important, and they were hopeful she would put her energy back into being an advocate in the States. Laura got a chance to see Daniela more as a person with insecurities like herself and not just as the always professional person she'd worked with. Both women learned that Antonio really was down to earth and sincere in his endeavors. They were both lucky to have made his acquaintance and befriend him.

"I'd like to make a toast. To friends. Thank you for your time, your assistance and support, and sharing your beautiful country. I look forward to positive outcomes going forward," offered Laura and they all touched bottles to glass.

After Laura finished cleaning the dinner dishes, she turned to Antonio. "I'd like to go for a walk. Can you join me or do you need to go? I'd like to give Daniela a little bit of quiet time. It's been a busy day for her."

"Not much I can do tonight. Where too?"

"How about we go check out the pool area? I haven't even had the chance to look it over or check out the grounds of the condo."

"That sounds like a nice idea. Daniela do you mind?" Antonio's butterflies flew in his gut.

"Not at all, I wouldn't mind a quick nap, it's been a busy day. Don't rush, by the way. Laura is right, I could use a little time alone," she said with a wink.

They walked to the pool making small talk along the way. "Will it be ok to come out here and sit by the pool while we're restricted in where we can go?" asked Laura.

"I would suggest letting Ignacio know so he can keep an eye on the area. You should be ok, but keep an eye on your surroundings and keep your phone handy so you can call Ignacio if need be. I'd prefer it if you and Daniela would come out together just for safety's sake. I don't want you to feel like a prisoner in your own home, but these guys apparently want to keep you and Daniela both quiet, so they're unpredictable."

***

They sat on the side of the pool with their feet dangling in the water. *Time to be bold.* Laura leaned over to kiss him on the cheek. "What was that for?" he asked.

"To thank you for getting Daniela to the hospital, rescuing us at the tunnel, and being available every time I needed to call. And, I think I have a crush on you," she replied as she felt a growing warmth on her cheeks and hung her head.

"I wasn't sure how to say this or if I even should, but I think I'm attracted to you too."

They stared at each other for a short time, both of their hearts raced. Then, Antonio moved to kiss her on her lips. She put her arms around his neck and the simple kiss turned into a much deeper kiss of longing. They knew then, when the chemistry sizzled between them, they would need to figure out what to do with it.

Chapter 40

The evening had been full of celebration, and the kiss made him want more. Laura was attractive, vulnerable, and determined at the same time. He'd felt arousal, missing for too long. The three Imperials he drank probably amplified that feeling.

The euphoria lasted until, at his own home, he put the key in his door and turned the lock. He reached in to flick the light switch. Nothing happened. Antonio stepped inside thinking a light was burnt out, but before he could close the door his arms were pinned from behind. On instinct, he head-butted the assailant. He bent to his center of gravity putting his right leg between the assailant's. As the intruder started to fall, Antonio kneed him in the stomach. To his right, unseen, a second assailant kicked Antonio's right knee, dropping him to the floor before punching the back of his neck. On his stomach, Antonio grabbed the second man's legs and pulled him down to the floor. They struggled until Antonio was able to sit on him and punch him into submission. He looked up, squinting.

The first assailant was standing over him gun aimed at his face. Antonio rolled to his right. A shot rang out and grazed Antonio's upper left arm. Antonio saw the handgun in the second attacker's waistband and grabbed it. He rolled on his back using the second man as cover and fired at the man near the doorway. Antonio heard a scream and saw the man grab his right arm as he ran from the house.

The odor of shot hung in the room and Antonio stood as he turned the gun on the second man.

"Move and you're dead."

The man froze. Even in the darkened room, his wide-eyed expression betrayed his fear. Antonio pulled his phone from his pocket, called for back up, and reached down to press the barrel to the man's forehead. With his free hand, unbuckled and removed the man's belt.

"Roll over," Antonio said. The man turned on to his stomach. Antonio bent his left knee into the man's spine as he secured the man's arms behind his back.

Antonio walked to his kitchen and wrapped a towel around his bleeding arm. Even in the fog of his adrenaline high, his mind assembled the police report. A different team would have to lead this new investigation. In his bones, he knew it related back to the kidnapping and drugs. He had a prisoner. *Now to get him to talk.* He hadn't gotten a good look at the other assailant.

When the team arrived, Antonio was driven to the nearby Hospital Rafael Ángel Calder Limónn Guardia. It looked like a nick, but didn't feel that way. The throbbing was bad, but he didn't want morphine. He needed to think straight and there was too much work to do to let this slow him down. He called his supervisor and told him what happened, relaying his suspicions. His supervisor sent a forensic team. *Damn. Another setback.*

***

The bullet grazed his arm but missed the humerus. The lost chunk of skin took ten sutures to close. Another scare, another notch, another story. The new OIJ members were able to get a couple of leads, and the name Wendigo surfaced again. Antonio was now certain that his attack was tied to the Playa Soledad murder and its investigation. However, he had no idea who Wendigo was, and Esteban's name wasn't mentioned. Antonio phoned Ignacio with a heads up at the Condo. He was driven to his mother's house to spent the evening there and recuperate. His home was now a crime scene.

***

The next day, arm wrapped in a thick dressing, he met with his supervisor. They had agreed that drug money had infiltrated the department and was highly likely affecting the evidence analysis.

"Any idea who these people in the lab are?" the supervisor asked.

183

"There are only two people I trust in the forensic lab," Antonio passed his supervisor the names. "I know these two will review the Playa Soledad findings thoroughly. If there is incomplete or misreported information in these cases, they will track it down and give us accurate information."

"The analysis of evidence and the DNA recovered should have been reported by now," his supervisor said. "This entire process is taking too long. Rafeal from MINAE phoned me earlier asking for updates. Apparently, the public is demanding answers too. He said something about future policy hinging on this investigation."

"Isn't that odd? OIJ is a separate branch of government. We don't report to the ministry. I thought they were supposed to wait for results and not interfere." Antonio said.

"You're right. That's why I'll assign the two individuals you requested. Something is going on here and I have confidence you're the one to find it."

Antonio made a mental note adding Rafeal Rodriguez as a possible contributor/benefactor of the drug money.

"Do you think we might be dealing with a cartel? Could this Wendigo character be the money source?" Antonio asked.

Several hours of analysis, theories, and requests continued. Finally, his boss said, "Go stay with your mother for a long weekend and rest. In the meantime, I'll have the team finish the forensic work at your house. I'll make sure the locks are changed and it's put under surveillance until the arrests are made. It'll be ready for your return on Monday."

**

Laura chose the black A-line dress she'd worn to Gabriel's funeral and was taking the opportunity to wear the matching lacey lingerie set she purchased on her last shopping trip. Although her skin was a little paler since she'd left the beach, the deep purple colors of the lingerie made her feel sexy. She was going to be seeing Antonio today and wanted to feel extra special. The black dress was the perfect topper. She wasn't sure if she was overdressed since this was a radio show, but it felt good to dress up, style her hair and put on eye makeup. She felt alive and energetic.

"Daniela, can you get that?" Her senses on high alert, Laura heard the knock at the front door even from the bathroom. "I'll be out in a minute." Her heart raced with anticipation, she hadn't seen Antonio since the night she made dinner. Her shaky hands made it hard to draw the liner on her eye lids.

"Okay, but you'd better hurry. You don't want to keep a good-looking guy waiting too long." Daniela teased as she rose from the sofa.

She stepped from the bathroom and made her way to the living area when she saw the bandage on his arm "What happened to you?" she asked.

"There was a little scuffle at my place a few nights ago. I was nicked by a bullet. Needed a few stitches, but no big deal."

Laura's eyes grew big and her voice reflected concern. "My god, that doesn't sound like a little scuffle to me. What happened?"

"When I got home, the night we had dinner here, a couple of guys were waiting for me. I was able to defend myself and arrest one of them. The OIJ's searching for the second guy. We've learned that they were given instructions by a suspect in Gabriel's case. I'm sure it's an attempt to stop the investigation. Now, I'm just more determined to find these people. Not to worry, my house is also under surveillance until we get these arrests made," Antonio responded. "Are you ready to go? It's about a 20-minute drive to get to the radio station by noon," he said with authority. Laura grabbed her small purse and headed to the door.

"Have fun, I know you'll do great. I can't wait to hear all about the experience, and I'll be listening to the broadcast," Daniela encouraged as they walked out the door.

Chapter 41

The host for the weekly radio talk show was gracious, and Laura found it interesting they focused on different areas of conservation within the country. The host prepped her - explaining the process and types of questions she could expect. She was comfortable with the experience, and felt accomplished pushing the conservation agenda forward.

As they were leaving, Antonio asked, "Do you mind if we quickly stop by my place? It's only fifteen minutes from here. I want to check on the new locks and make sure it's habitable again."

Her heart raced. *A chance to be alone with him, this is great.* "That would be nice, I'd like to see where you live." She blushed and fidgeted with her hands.

They drove to his house and looked around. Nothing appeared suspicious. A couple of cars were parked along the street up three houses from his. In one, a person behind the wheel reviewed a map. Or so it seemed. No police cars were in the area.

"Is everything in place?" Laura asked as he scanned the street. He was a bit apprehensive about bringing Laura here, but knew it would be his only chance to have a few moments alone with her. He didn't want to rush anything. The kiss they shared led him to believe there was more passion to be uncovered.

"Everything appears to be normal," he said as he opened the truck door for her.

He unlocked his house's door, peered inside. Everything had been straightened and fingerprint dust removed. He invited her to sit on the sofa while he checked the rooms. He was on alert, anxious because he had a beautiful woman in his home, and feeling those damn butterflies churning his stomach again. All was quiet.

Doors and windows shut and locked. He appreciated the extra effort the supervisor had given to make sure his home was clean.

"Would you like a quick tour?" he asked moving back toward Laura.

She glanced at the beautiful wooden table with the deep tones of reddish brown in the swirls of wood, but the living area was sparse. The look signaled "bachelor" to her.

"I'd love to. Nice table, the swirls are intriguing," she responded.

He offered his hand to help her up from the leather sofa. They made their way through the kitchen and the two bedrooms and one bath.

"Did you add the wood floors? Most of the homes I've seen in Limón had concrete or ceramic floors."

"I did, put them in myself." Pride shown on his face.

His bedroom had a masculine feel. Dark wood headboard and matching side table with drawers. The bed was neatly made and the walls were a soft buttery shade that complimented the dark wood.

They stood in the doorway of his bedroom. Laura felt a little embarrassed and awkward and yet a tingle of sensation moved south. She'd envisioned this moment in her mind several times and she needed to make a move now or they could lose the moment. She put her hand behind his neck and pulled him close to kiss him. That kiss of longing they'd felt before reappeared. She felt her breasts swell inside her bra as she moved her hand to his chest. She could feel the firmness of his muscles through his dark grey blue t-shirt and anticipated the muscle definition under it.

He cupped her breasts through her dress as they kissed harder moving toward his bed. The mattress hit the back of her knees and she sat and untucked his shirt from his jeans and made her way toward the metal button and zipper. Her dress fell from her shoulders exposing her purple and black lacy bra. Their kissing became more urgent.

She gently removed his shirt not wanting to hurt his arm and tugged his jeans down towards his hips. *God he is as beautiful as I had imagined,* she thought. She wriggled out of her dress, and exposed her matching lace panties that hugged her firm hips.

Laura climbed atop Antonio. Her honey blonde hair, shimmering in a daylight slipping through the blinds, cascaded long and loose over her shoulders.

He had a tattoo on his chest over his heart. A Latin cross. Each arm of the cross had a scalloped edge and at the center was a heart in the shape of angel's wings. There was a teardrop above the heart. Her fingers followed its outline. "This is beautiful. What does it mean?" She kissed it.

"I had that done after my brother died. A Latin cross will bring good luck and deliver one from evil. The wings are a symbol of my brother watching over me from heaven."

His sensitivity moved her. She traced the six dimples on his abdominals knowing he worked out often. Her fingers kept moving as she took him in her hands. He was ready.

She could tell he was having a hard time with the clasps on her bra using only one hand so she stopped to help. She felt an electric charge run through her as he played with her breasts and she lowered herself to him.

She liked being on top, it made her feel powerful, sexy, in control. She moved her lips to his neck, his ears, and stroked his chest as she fell into a rhythm with his hips. They both reached the pinnacle together and then nested in each other's arms. Laura even forgot about her ribs, she felt peaceful in his arms. He felt protective of her.

"How are you feeling?" Antonio asked as he gazed into her radiant face.

"Mmm."

"It wasn't my intent to take advantage of you, bringing you here."

"You didn't take advantage of me. If I remember correctly, I made the first move. I hoped you would reciprocate." Laura smiled while she carefully rolled to her right side and propped herself up on her elbow circling his belly button with her left index finger. "That was magical." She grinned as she leaned over to kiss him again. "I haven't felt those feelings in so long I thought they were lost within the depths of me. You've brought me back to life." Antonio blushed at the statement.

"Now what?"

"Well, I guess we better get back to the condo or Daniela will have the police looking for us, don't you think?" She giggled.

"I meant what about us, this thing that just happened between us? I don't want this to be a onetime thing. I'm really attracted to you. I want to know you, who you are." He sat up to meet her face.

"Why do we have to worry about that now? Let's just enjoy the last couple of weeks I have here. I don't want this to be a onetime thing either."

"I guess," he reluctantly agreed and stood to dress.

Chapter 42

"You sounded terrific on the radio." Daniela placed a plate of sliced pineapple on the kitchen island as Laura and Antonio entered the condo.

"Thanks, I had a lot of fun. I learned a lot about *Rainforest Radio's* mission and was happy to answer Renee's questions. She's passionate about conservation efforts in Costa Rica. I bet we could get her to join the march tomorrow—she can report about it on her next show. I'll call her and ask."

"That would be nice. By the way, I thought you would have been back about an hour ago, did you guys stop for lunch?" Daniela eyed them with a knowing grin.

"I had a few errands to run. Laura agreed to join me while we were in the area," Antonio said.

"Oh, I see," Daniela saw Laura blush.

"The radio show was exciting but I needed to catch my breath, so the errands helped." Laura nervously looked away from Daniela. "The MINAE meeting and the walk from there to OIJ is tomorrow, do you think you'll be up to it?"

"I'm sure I'll be fine. I'm looking forward to it and hope we can make some progress this time."

"Good."

"While you were out, I drafted a new proposal. I have a Plan B if we can't get Playa Soledad to be a national park. Maybe we can get it designated a protected area during nesting season? It would be a compromise to my initial request and I'm confident I can get other local agencies on board. I might be able to get some local businesses to agree to support this also."

Daniela was at her laptop, keyboard clicking beneath her fingers. "I've been sending out emails for the last hour. I know I'm cutting it close to tomorrow's activities. I'm really excited about this one. I feel it's reasonable and can work for all parties involved. I'm ready to start the phone calls as a follow up to the emails. I'd love to go into that meeting with this in final edit and with a list of supporters behind me. I still need to call the Limón business owners and encourage them to attend again as well."

"That sounds wonderful. I'll help with the calls. It's great to see your enthusiasm come back, but don't overdo it—we need you fresh tomorrow. Do you want to give me part of your list? I'll sit on the terrace with my cell phone," said Laura.

"I'd appreciate that. Let me pull some information for you."

"Sounds like you ladies will be busy; I'll go check on Ignacio."

"Antonio, will you be driving us to the meeting tomorrow? It's at 2." Laura watched his face.

"I have it on my calendar, and unless something unexpected arises, I'll be here. When would you like the chauffer to arrive?" He smiled in good humor.

"One fifteen would be good, I want to be sure we are up front again. Thank you." Daniela added her two cents.

Antonio headed toward the door.

Laura stood from the bar stool and met him at the door. "Let me see you out." She closed the door behind them. "Thank you for a wonderful afternoon." She kissed him again. "I look forward to seeing you tomorrow."

"Me too, bye for now." Antonio gave her one last kiss and walked away.

Laura took a deep breath, gathered herself and headed back inside hoping she wouldn't get more questions from Daniela.

"I see you two are getting along." Daniela grinned.

"Um, yes. He is very nice you know. Polite. And, in case you missed it, he's damn HOT. Might I add quite the kisser too. Now if you have that list ready, I'm going to go swoon over my new crush while I assist you with phone calls. Any objections?" Laura put her hand on her hip. Her little outburst surprised herself.

"I guess not," said Daniela taken aback with Laura's candidness. "I've just sent a partial list to your email with the draft of the proposal to give you an idea of what to say. Remind them about the meeting and the OIJ walk then confirm their attendance. Don't forget to ask for their support on the proposal. I'd like a headcount from Limón. I'll contact the other conservation agencies."

"Will do." Lara grabbed a glass of ice water, and walked to the terrace.

***

Alonso had been parked down the street in the blue Corolla. This time he parked near a home with the car's hood up and pretended to work on the engine. He watched as the new security detail patrolled the condo premises, but felt he blended into the neighborhood so well no one would notice him. He would walk to the local businesses near the condo and back to the car. He watched Laura and Antonio come and go, but hadn't followed. He hoped Daniela would leave and was disappointed when she hadn't.

Alonso had put the word out that he needed a room to rent in the area and someone had contacted him. An older woman advertised for a roommate that would help her take care of her home. There was a second bedroom with a window view onto the condo from the opposite angle he'd been at. Perfect. He could still keep an eye on them and movement around the home would give him more opportunity. It would be far more comfortable than being cramped in a vehicle all day.

The neighborhood had its rhythm, a time when everyone would be leaving for their jobs or school, a time for conversing with families and neighbors and of course siesta time in the heat of the day. He'd use this. He was surprised no one had called him out for sitting in a car all day. It seemed no one paid attention to anything that didn't involve them directly. His last conversation with Esteban informed him of the pending MINAE meeting with everyone who was expected to attend. Alonso was to be there too, Esteban wanted a report on what Señor Rodriguez's agenda contained, specifically information regarding the investigation of the murder.

Chapter 43

Laura woke with pain in her ribs that she'd ignored yesterday. Today was the MINAE meeting and she had to attend. She wanted justice for Gabriel before she left. Nothing a strong cup of coffee and a good breakfast couldn't help her through. She got up from the sofa, hit the cold shower and marched on.

Daniela was brewing coffee as Laura came from the bathroom. Her long brown hair was up in a bun, and she wore a turquoise sheath dress. Laura thought she looked bright, alert, professional and beautiful all at the same time.

"You look confident this morning," Laura said.

"Thank you. I'm thrilled about today and am sure the turnouts going to be great. It's good to be back in the fight."

Laura had chosen the hounds-tooth blouse and black slim skirt she wore to the first meeting, but freshened the look with a dark tank underneath. She wore the shirt open like a jacket.

"What's the plan for today? Do you think Señor Rodriguez will question me this time, or should I just speak up regardless?" Laura scrambled a couple of eggs, sliced half a mango and poured her coffee.

"I think it'll depend on the atmosphere and turnout at the meeting. I've notified his office of my new proposal so they'll allow a few minutes for me to speak. I'd like to include your statement in my presentation that way we don't give him a choice. Do you think you can highlight your work as a volunteer, the relationship with Gabriel and the surprise of the kidnapping in a succinct ten minutes? I'm thinking this would be a good lead into the compromise I want to offer about protection through turtle season," Daniela said, "I just thought of it this morning while making the coffee so I know I haven't given you much time to prepare."

"I've recounted that moment so many times. I'll jot some notes down just as soon as I'm done eating. We have plenty of time before Antonio arrives. I'm glad you had the coffee ready when I finished with my shower. I think this could be a four-cup kind of morning," Laura said.

"How are your ribs feeling? You seem to be favoring that side."

"It's most bothersome after I've been sleeping all night. Once I get up and start moving it's tolerable. I try to ignore it. I have too much on my mind, and we have so much to do yet. Thanks for asking though."

***

Antonio arrived promptly at 1:15 p.m. He looked handsome as always dressed in a metal-grey, two-button business suit, his hair slicked back, his five o'clock shadow trimmed. Neither woman had ever seen him dressed so formally.

"Wow, you look nice. Very cosmopolitan. Why exactly?" Daniela teased.

"Funny, I just came from an important meeting with my supervisor and senior OIJ staff. The occasion called for a business suit. I didn't have time to change and be here to get you on time, so this is what you get," he said with a smile. "The good news is, we've made changes in the forensic team and we're finally getting the long overdue results. I had a chance to share a plan regarding possible arrests. But, to carry it out, it will still be a couple more weeks. I wish I could tell you more."

His suit was European slim cut and Laura thought *Damn, he looks like a GQ model.* Out of selfishness, she wanted to take him back to the States and show him off. *Curious how some of life's unexpected tragic events lead to fresh starts and new friendships.*

"You ladies look quite handsome yourself. Are you ready to go?"

"Yes, we are," Daniela said as she put her notes and folder into her shoulder bag.

***

"It's Rafael. I've just learned that there has been a forensic team change. The team we had is being relieved of their duties due to

194

the delays in reporting. Señor De La Torres is the one that made the request. I'd asked for an update for today's meeting with the group from Limón, but the OIJ won't release that to me. They're being tight lipped with information. I don't know what they know or what their next actions will be, but they've cut cooperation with our office."

"I see," Wendigo said.

"I'll reconfirm to the group what I've said before. We suspect two individuals and should have arrests by next week. This should be enough to keep them quiet and settle the media."

"Thank you. I'm not getting new information from my team either. We must make our next moves carefully, and assume they have information not favorable to us." Wendigo's voice held a frown.

***

The MINAE meeting was in a different room, one just as sterile as the first. The trio grabbed seats in the second row this time. Alonso took up his post in the back of the room. The front row was full of journalists and TV cameras. Rafael Rodriguez Salas entered the room. His presence was more commanding this time and reminiscent of a politician. He was again joined by the MSP.

Rafael made his opening address, acknowledged each group in attendance and set out the agenda for the meeting. The Limón businesses were the first to speak, still angered by the continued loss of business experienced since Gabriel's murder. "We're concerned with the lack of law enforcement overall in Limón," said one business owner.

"We are in the process of addressing that. We've added to the budget to allow for more hires currently in training and they will be assigned as soon as possible," the MSP interrupted.

Several environmental groups from around the country spoke about their experiences facing hostile conditions in the areas they worked, and these were in addition to the turtle egg poaching concerns. They demanded that current park security officers also be armed and trained to make arrests. One conservation group presented a video in honor of Gabriel encouraging the boycott of turtle eggs. An advertising agency presented their new campaign video showing a beautiful bikini clad Tica talking about turtle hatchlings, along with a sexy print ad discouraging the myth of turtle eggs as an aphrodisiac, and demanded an end to turtle poaching.

Finally Daniela's turn. "Costa Rica has marketed itself globally as a pro-conservation country encouraging volunteerism and environmentally minded tourists to spend their money here. I want to introduce you to one of those volunteers." She summarized Laura's story and used her time to ask Laura questions so the audience and Señor Rodriguez could hear the truth from her, understand the relationships she built with Gabriel, her host family, and the other volunteers.

Laura recounted the night of the kidnapping again. The audience fell silent as Laura did her best in Spanish to relay the fear and surprise of such a simple deed being interrupted by drug traffickers.

Daniella continued, "Gabriel had requested protection for himself numerous times but was denied. Señor Rodriguez, you will recall that I had previously requested that Playa Soledad become a national park. However, you said that new development planned in the area makes this request impossible. I have a compromise to suggest. With the support of the Limón businesses, the increased police force promised by the MSP, Playa Soledad could be deemed a protected area during turtle nesting season.

"A smaller section of the beach where the largest percentage of nesting occurs would be included. The community will create a tourist event to celebrate the nesting season, which would bring seasonal jobs to many and displace the poaching. This could be accomplished safely and would be a chance to educate tourists on the plight of all sea turtles, while controlling a tourist footprint that could damage the nesting areas."

The crowd applauded her speech.

"Thank you Señorita Segura for that very passionate plea. I will take it under consideration as many of your ideas seem to be sound and you have Limón business support. I would also like to declare that MINAE will celebrate the memory of Gabriel Montenegro and his contribution to Costa Rican conservation by honoring him at the 50th Anniversary of the National Park System later this year."

Rafael also assured the Limón business contingent that they were working quickly to help make arrests and bring business back to the region.

The business groups, environmentalists, Antonio, Daniela and Laura met in front of the MINAE building. They gathered their signs and banners and with Daniela in the lead started the three-hundred-meter walk to the OIJ Building. They repeated their usual chants *"¡Queremos arrestos!"* calling for arrests in Gabriel's murder.

Daniela, megaphone in hand, shared the news that 137,000 signatures from 150 nations had been signed on a petition created by *Seaturtle.org* in the U.S. to protect turtle beaches. Those signatures had been delivered to the Costa Rican Consulate in California on this day. Everyone cheered.

"I call for a global protest of all conservation agencies to meet again in front of their capitol buildings on 15 July, if no arrests have been made in the Playa Soledad murder and kidnappings," Daniela shouted.

A few other conservation groups and business leaders used the megaphone to keep the crowd energized. The group assembled for an hour and then disbanded.

Everyone's adrenaline increased. Daniela and Laura were satisfied with the meeting and thrilled with the turnout. They felt the people of Costa Rica on their side and the pressure was where they wanted it. The trio celebrated with cocktails at Barrio Pura Vida, the interior reminding Laura of a bar in San Francisco. They joined the after work crowd, and rock music played in the background. Laura celebrated this new-found energy with a stiff and generous mojito.

Chapter 44

Four weeks without an arrest in the Playa Soledad Murder, and Laura's sabbatical was running out of time. Her body reminded her that she was still recovering from the injury but she knew she had another four weeks on her travel visa.

"Laura, are you ok? You looked lost in thought," Daniela said as they sat on the terrace with their morning coffee.

"I'm fine, just lots going through my head. I'm sad because I have to leave soon, and I need to make a decision about exactly when. I've been receiving emails and phone messages from work pressuring me to come back and they're threatening to replace my position. I really hate this corporate hassle, but I need my job in the short term until I can make other choices. I was hoping to spend more time with Antonio, and wish arrests were made already."

"Do you think you could extend your travel a couple more weeks? The last group of turtles Gabriel saved will be ready to hatch then. It would be nice to have you there to watch them get to sea. One last memorial to Gabriel," Daniela suggested.

"Going back to Limón would allow me to say goodbye to the Valverdes and visit Gabriel's grave one last time." Laura swirled her coffee mug looking into the dark liquid. "Here's what I'll do, I'll plan to leave by July 13th, arrests or not. I'll call my employer and let them know." Next she had to break the news to Antonio.

***

The new forensics team worked overtime reviewing notes and re-testing evidence where possible. DNA tests had come back on the blood found at the Pocora ranch and results linked it to Luis Rodriguez Salas. The hair sample found on the body came back to one Esteban Rojas Madrigal. Antonio received the report and was ecstatic to have two names. He knew Esteban and Luis. *Excellent,* he thought, *the hair ties Esteban to the murder and the blood ties Luis to the drug processing at the ranch. Now I just need to connect the drug processing to the kidnapping and murder.*

After four weeks, Antonio corroborated a portion of the Playa Soledad kidnapping and murder story told by Manuel Jimenez Calderon. He was certain the men involved would be working with Esteban at the Pacuare rafting outfitter. He wanted to snag everyone at once and thought scheduling a corporate trip could be a workable decoy.

He had his supervisor's secretary make the call using an alias company name, and booked a trip for 20 to improve the chances all suspects would be there.

"I'll need two teams for arrests. One with me to assist with the arrests at the river company, and a second team outside of the suspects homes in case they aren't with the group." Antonio said to his supervisor as the secretary beeped in.

"The fingerprints for the AK-47 just came back. Forensics said they belong to Pedro Villalobos Tres. They were able to make a comparison with the cell phone he handled," said the secretary.

"Gracias, Rita." His supervisor smiled at Antonio.

"If we make simultaneous arrests of Esteban, Luis, Pedro, and Alonso, we'll have four of the five men Manuel named in his confession. We'll get preventative detention and hold them while we continued to make this case. I'll still have one man to locate. We can use suspicion of kidnapping and accessory for the arrests at Pacuare River Rafting Adventures. If we get every employee there that day we'd have more suspects to question which could help solidify the investigation."

Antonio felt his phone vibrate in his pocket. "De La Torres."

"It's Miguel from forensics. I wanted to let you know the fingerprints from the laptop and sliding door were two different sets and we could not find them on record."

"*¡Maldita sea!*" Antonio said. Another setback.

"We did learn there are two current addresses listed for an Alonso Mendez Morales and one happens to be very close to the condo where you placed security. This address did not come up in an earlier search, so it's recent," Miguel said.

"What's the second address?" Antonio motioned for a piece of paper and something to write with. He took the information and stood.

"This is an arrest I need to make immediately," he explained to his supervisor. "I'll need a backup. Can you have someone you trust meet me downstairs?"

***

Antonio parked near the condo to avoid suspicion, and observed the area for a few moments, no movement. He dialed Ignacio's phone, "Anything unusual in the area since we last spoke?"

"No. The streets have been quiet, not a lot of people moving about. It's too hot," Ignacio said.

Antonio and his backup were within 100 yards of the house Alonso had reported as his address. Antonio made his way toward the condo; taking the lead, his backup walked toward the house.

Antonio moved slowly around one of the condo buildings allowing himself to be in second position. The policía knocked on the door and a woman answered.

"How can I help you?" she said.

"I'm looking for Alonso Mendez Morales," he said.

"He's in his room, I'll go get him."

Across the street, Antonio scanned additional areas where someone could exit. Sure enough, he spotted Alonso climbing through the bedroom window. Antonio ran toward the window with his gun raised and had it pointed at him before the suspect was completely out. Once Alonso was cuffed, hands behind his back, Antonio called for his backup.

"Alonso Mendez Morales, you're under arrest for suspicion of stalking, stolen goods and falsifying information. You're coming with us," Antonio said. They pushed him into the backseat of Antonio's truck, the second officer sat next to him for the ride back to OIJ. Alonso would be held there until other arrangements could be made.

Back at his desk, Antonio called Daniela. "I wanted to let you know we received the results of the fingerprints taken from your condo. I just arrested a suspect linked to the kidnapping and

200

murder. This person... has been renting a room down the street from you."

"I have shivers down my spine. To know someone from that group was so close all along is unsettling. I'll update Laura. I assume you'll be busy for a while."

"Yes. Please let her know I'll call when I have a moment," he said and hung up.

***

A day passed without hearing from Antonio, so Laura made the call.

"Hi. Daniela told me about the arrest you made yesterday. We're happy to hear you got him, not sure I understand why we still have to have protection though."

"I'm sure he has been working with others connected to your kidnapping. I'm still working on that. We're getting closer to making arrests but until that happens, I would feel better if you both stayed where we can keep an eye on you. If drugs are involved, these people can be ruthless. I want you to get home safely."

"About that, I've made a decision. I'm leaving in two weeks. My job is calling me back." Laura bit her lower lip, then continued, "I was wondering if you were available this weekend? I'll have been here eight weeks on Saturday. I was hoping we could do something fun outside of this investigation before I leave."

"What did you have in mind?" Antonio felt nervous excitement bubbling in his stomach.

"It would be nice to have an actual date. You know, dinner, a movie, something like that. Do you dance? I loved the nightclub I went to in Limón. It would be fun to visit one in San José before I go. You could be my bodyguard. I'm sure Daniela wouldn't mind a little time to herself," Laura felt her cheeks warm.

"I think we could manage that. I have an idea. There's a place called El Pueblo, it's a collection of restaurants, bars, and dance clubs. We could try one and walk to another. I would suggest starting at Las Brisas for dinner. Cumbia is a nightclub with live

201

bands on Saturday nights. There are several other discothèques with different types of music we could try that are also in the area."

"That sounds perfect. What time will you pick me up?" she asked.

"I'll pick you up at 7."

"Sounds good. I'm eager to explore the city before I leave. I hear San José nightlife is legendary."

"Great. I'll see you then."

Chapter 45

Wendigo rang Esteban. "Have you heard the news?"

"What news?"

"Rafael called, said one of your men was arrested for stalking the Segura condo. They have also added stolen goods. Have you not been in touch with your men?"

"We just spoke yesterday. His last report was that everything was quiet. No one had left the condo and a security guard had been watching over them." Esteban sat straight from his slouched position.

"Esteban, there are too many loose ends. What are you going to do about it?"

The calmness in Wendigo's voice unsettled Esteban.

"I'll think of something. Where are they detaining him?"

"He's in a holding cell at OIJ. He's been there since yesterday afternoon." This time his voice was colder.

"Those holding cells are so overcrowded, I'm sure someone on the inside can get me additional information. There's a high probability he could encounter violence while he waits to be moved. I'll make a couple of phone calls."

"Get this under control. We're losing money daily. I'm going to have to get innovative in moving product to Mexico without you. You've become a liability to this partnership." Wendigo's anger was palpable when he ended the conversation. Esteban's face reddened with fury as he threw his half-filled highball glass against the wall.

***

Laura wore her favorite yellow halter dress one more time. She'd placed her long honey blonde hair up in a loose Gibson tuck which softened her face and gave her a romantic look in combination with the dress. Her skin was golden once again from time near the pool and the bright yellow against her skin made it glow. She was excited about the date. Being around music would be a relief from so much seriousness. She hoped it would be with a Latin flare, and a chance to move closer to Antonio. With any luck, this evening would end up at his place again. She thought she had lost that feeling forever after her divorce, but Antonio relit her fire.

He was prompt as usual. He wore dark indigo skinny jeans, and a pale blue cotton button down shirt with the sleeves rolled to three quarter length. He had shaved his five o'clock shadow, making his face smooth, angular and gorgeous. The beard made him appear much more intimidating. "I hope you're ready for tonight. Costa Ricans love to dance and we love our music loud," he said.

"I'm ready. I love music and can't wait to move to it. Can we try the merengue? I haven't done that since dancing with Gabriel. It'll be good to remember him with music." They said their goodbyes to Daniela and with any luck hoped they'd be out all night.

***

The restaurant, with white tablecloths and fabric covered chairs, had a host who seated them at a table for two facing out on El Pueblo. The lights in the area and around the walkways sparkled as they reflected off the wet concrete. *Very romantic ambiance. So far so good*, she thought. Antonio ordered a pricey bottle of an imported Chilean Chardonnay, "Ticos love a good Chilean wine, so I hope you'll enjoy this."

"I'm sure I will."

The waiter came by and Antonio ordered for them. "We'll have the Mahi Mahi."

"Good choice, sir," the waiter replied.

"I hope you don't mind that I ordered for you? The fresh fish here is highly rated, so I want to be sure you have a good experience." Antonio looked into Laura's grey blue eyes while he settled his napkin on his lap.

"That's fine. I love Mahi Mahi."

They sat across from one another and Antonio just kept staring into her eyes—she was attracted to him but was feeling a little

204

uncomfortable at the same time. "Is there something wrong with my hair, do I have a mascara smudge? You keep staring at me," Laura asked.

"No, I'm sorry, I don't mean to stare. You're so beautiful, your eyes are hypnotizing to me," he said in a low sexy voice.

"Wow. That's the nicest compliment anyone has given me." Laura blushed, "You're quite the charmer, aren't you?" She demurely tilted her chin, her heart raced, and she felt warmth in a couple other areas.

Following dinner, they stopped for a short time at Cumbia, but the band wasn't playing Latin inspired music so Laura wanted to find another disco.

"I have an idea. If Salsa is what you want, let's go to Discotheque Castro. That dance floor is always lively," Antonio said.

"That sounds wonderful. The variety at El Pueblo is great, but it seems a little touristy to me. I'd like to visit a place that's popular with Ticos."

"Then Discotheque Castro it is." Antonio put his hand on her back and lead her to his truck.

***

The disco was loud, crowded, and had a combination of strong floral perfume mixed with woodsy, smoky scents that filled the air. The music was what Laura had hoped for. *They even have a disco ball. Perfect*, she thought. Antonio taught her a Salsa move, and they tried the Merengue again so she wouldn't forget the steps Gabriel taught her. They danced for a couple of hours.

"This has been so much, fun. Can we find a table? I need to take a short break." Laura tried to tuck stray strands of hair back into her up-do.

Antonio found a couple of stools at the bar, and ordered drinks.

"Are you ready to leave, or do you want to dance again?" Antonio finished his beer.

"Actually, can we go back to your place?" Laura asked sheepishly. "It's so quiet there, and there's no Daniela to bump into. I don't want this night to end, just need it to slow down."

"Sure, if that's what you want to do." Antonio controlled the smile he felt.

"It is. Besides, I told Daniela I'd be out all night. It'd be easier to talk, we haven't really done much of that tonight, and I leave soon. I have so many questions I want to ask you."

"Let's go." Antonio took her hand ushering her from the disco. He hoped she was thinking what he was thinking as his heart rate sped up.

Chapter 46

Alsonso woke for a second time in the cramped OIJ cell. He huddled in a corner as far away as possible from his menacing cell mates. He hadn't implicated anyone in the kidnappings but confessed to the stalking once they told him they had his fingerprints on record and proved he was at the condo.

A guard approached the cell. "Alonso Mendez Morales" he called.

"Yes," Alonso scrambled to his feet and walked toward the guard.

"I have a message for you."

Alonso leaned forward and grabbed the bars, "What is it?"

The guard pushed a knife deep into Alonso's abdomen and said, "Esteban sends his regrets."

Alonso's eyes widened as he sucked in a breath. The guard shouted something, angering the prisoners. A fight broke out, Alonso dropped to the ground.

***

The morning sun crept in through the window blinds. Laura was asleep in the fetal position on her left side. Antonio mirrored her position, his arm wrapped around her waist. His cell phone rang waking them both. He rolled over. "What? How?" was all Laura heard him say, "I'll be there as soon as I can," he ended the call. "I'm afraid I've got to get you back home; I need to go into OIJ today. The suspect we arrested the other day has been stabbed. They don't think he'll make it."

"Oh no. What happened?"

"They aren't sure. The holding cell he was in was overcrowded and a fight broke out. Apparently, another suspect stabbed him several times. No one knows where the knife came from. I'm guessing someone didn't want him talking. I've got to get over there as soon as possible." They both jumped up, dressed, and headed out the door.

***

A week passed and Antonio was busy with multiple cases, eager to get the arrests made in the Playa Soledad murder.

Laura played tourist her last couple of weeks, with Daniela as her guide. They'd convinced Ignacio to come with them as security, and he would conduct a condo check upon their return. They shopped downtown San José so Laura could pick up trinkets for her friends and family. They spent a day at the La Paz Waterfall Garden tour. Their friendship had grown into a sisterhood. They planned a weekend trip to Manuel Antonio Nature Preserve on the Pacific side of the country. Laura had wanted to visit there on her first trip but ran out of time and she was determined to get there this time. She hoped Antonio could take a couple of days to join them.

***

Antonio's final plans for the company river rafting adventure at Pacuare River Tours was coming together. A couple more days and he would have everyone in custody. He lined up a dozen men for his rafting team, and another six to be stationed at the homes of Esteban, Luis, Beni, and Pedro as back up. The day would be July 8, six weeks after Gabriel's murder. He even rented one of the tour company's olive green buses to alleviate any suspicion.

***

The day arrived. Everyone was in place.

Antonio and his team were dressed and ready for river rafting. As the bus approached the facility, Antonio met with his men. "I need each of you to survey an area. Here are the pictures of the suspects. You need to find them and implement the plan for containing them. You have fifteen minutes from the time Esteban gives us the initial instructions. Meet back here," he said.

Esteban greeted the van and didn't see Antonio in the group. "Welcome to Pacuare River Tours," he greeted them. "We have an

208

exhilarating trip planned for you today." Esteban showed them where to find the lockers and suggested putting their belongings there prior to the safety briefing.

The men moved about and followed directions. Antonio kept his head down under a baseball cap as he searched for the other suspects.

Weapons were stashed in their backpacks.

They reported back that Pedro was stationed at the photo center, Luis at the café, and a third man in the gift shop. Antonio hoped it would be Beni. "I need each of you to take your back packs toward the lockers, but keep your weapons handy. Once Esteban starts the safety meeting you'll arrest those men in their current locations. I want Esteban."

Esteban made the announcement to meet back at the bus for the safety talk and to get life vests. A small group of men moved toward him, Antonio hiding among them. Esteban began his speech.

Following orders, the first officer approached Luis. "I'd like a cup of coffee," the officer said.

"Sir, we are not open yet. You need to be in the safety meeting taking place right now," Luis said.

"Luis Rodrigues Salas, you are under arrest for possession of an illegal firearm, suspicion of processing cocaine, stalking, kidnapping and assault, and accessory to murder." The first officer said. Luis took off towards the back of the park. He jumped over a bush, and rolled his ankle. The officer closed in on him just as Luis went down, rolled him to his stomach, and cuffed his hands behind his back.

Pedro approached the second officer. "Mister, I think you're lost, you should be over there at the safety meeting." Pedro pointed to the larger group.

"Are you Pedro Villalobos Tres?" he asked.

"Yes, who's asking?" said Pedro

"You are under arrest for kidnapping, stolen goods and accessory to murder," the official said pointing his gun at Pedro. "Now turn around."

Pedro threw a small box at the officer, looking around for something to use as a weapon. The cop got off a round but missed.

Pedro ran for the door as he hurled a small camera, missing the officer who propelled himself at Pedro, tackling and cuffing him.

Esteban heard the commotion and looked around. "If you will excuse me, I seem to be needed near the café," he started to turn and walk away. Antonio moved forward gun leveled as Esteban's chest.

"Esteban Rojas Madrigal, you are under arrest for the murder of Gabriel Montenegro, kidnapping, and suspicion of trafficking illegal substances."

"You're mistaken." Esteban lurched for Antonio's gun, trying to knock it from his hands. To avoid Esteban's hand, Antonio stepped to his right and kicked Esteban's leg with his left foot. They both tumbled to the ground and the gun fell away. Esteban threw a right hook at Antonio's face, but Antonio blocked it. They wrestled for a few seconds before Antonio punched Esteban in the left ear. As Esteban reached to grab his ear, Antonio grabbed his arm, rolled him to his stomach and cuffed his arms behind him. Two officers ran to Antonio's aid, helped him to his feet and restrained Esteban. While Antonio and Esteban wrestled, two other members of Antonio's team approached Beni as he was refilling a bin with toys and arrested him for kidnapping, processing cocaine, drug trafficking and accessory to murder. Beni did not resist. The men were loaded into the bus and driven back to OIJ holding cells. Bail was set at 500,000 colones each and they were immediately given six-month detention so legal staff assigned could prepare the case against them. With the men in custody, Antonio hoped he would learn the identity of the mysterious Wendigo.

Antonio called the media outlets himself to report the news of multiple arrests in the murder of conservationist and biologist Gabriel Montenegro. He also called Laura and Daniela to let them know the arrests were made and Ignacio could be relieved of his duties. They would have their freedom back.

***

With his largest case now closed, Antonio was finally able to take a break. He knew that Laura and Daniela were headed to Manuel Antonio National Park. He hoped Laura still wanted him to join them, but they hadn't spoken in several days. He booked a room at their hotel and called her on his way there.

"I would love to see you. We'll have a chance to catch up before I have to leave," Laura said.

"I've booked my own room. Do you think Daniela will be upset if you were to join me?"

"I doubt it. Turns out she had a little surprise for me. Apparently she and Ignacio have a little thing going so he's joined us. Your timing is perfect. How soon can you be here?"

"I'm on my way as we speak."

***

Nicholas Herrera inspected the new crew of children expected to work in his apparel factory in Barranquilla, Colombia when he heard the news. The talk radio station reported the arrests of four suspects in the murder of the conservationist at Playa Soledad. The reporters identified the men and said OIJ was looking for a person of interest with the nickname Wendigo, thought to be the financier of the group.

Nicholas coughed as he heard the news. "Please excuse me. Get these new employees trained on the sewing machines immediately. We must meet production quotas," he said to the foreman as he stepped away to the conference room.

He knew Esteban was the only person that could connect him to Wendigo but was confident that Esteban would know the consequence of ratting him out. Wendigo was the name Nicholas used in Costa Rica and only with the drug trade. He had several others based on business he was conducting. Although his business in Costa Rica had been interrupted, he was still earning large profits in child trafficking. He used the children as mules to get his product to Mexico bypassing Costa Rica altogether. Esteban was now a liability; a call was made.

"I have a project for you. I need someone you can trust to take care of a little problem in Costa Rica. This someone will have no problem getting past OIJ authorities. I don't want to know who you send, nor are they to know who gave the order. I am putting a large sum of money into the account we previously agreed to," Wendigo said to his contact at a private security company as he gave the kill order for Esteban.

Chapter 47

With only a couple of days left in Costa Rica, Laura packed for one last visit to Puerto Limón with Daniela. They would meet the Valverdes for dinner at the best Caribbean restaurant in the area, Laura's treat as a final thank you for everyone's support and friendship.

The following morning, they witnessed the arrival of the 100 hatchlings at the Playa Soledad hatchery that Gabriel saved prior to his death. The baby turtles popped from the sand one after another like popcorn out of a hot pan. Laura picked up a couple of hatchlings, two filled her palm. She helped with the process of DNA testing and tagging so their progress could be followed.

"It's amazing to think that these little guys, surviving all the challenges ahead of them, will become one of the largest sea turtles ever seen." Laura glanced at the horizon imagining their future size. Once the tagging was complete, Daniela, Laura, the Valverdes, and some additional local volunteers created a barrier to help them make their way to the water's edge. They named the first turtle that appeared from the sand Gabriel, and they looked on as he led the others to the surf.

Daniela gathered the troops. "Thank you everyone for coming today. It's bittersweet releasing the last of these hatchlings. I want to share a new idea for the Leatherback Sea Turtle Conservancy. Since I'm not confident in bringing foreign volunteers back to this beach, I thought it'd be great to make Francisco and Orlando tour guides for conservation tourism. They'll lead tours featuring information on the leatherback sea turtles at Playa Soledad, avoiding the now notorious north shore. This gives them an opportunity to teach others about the plight of the sea turtles and will put more money in their pocket than the poaching. In addition, this goal will help increase the tourist visits to Puerto Limón where local businesses will also benefit, leading to better jobs for residents."

"That's a great idea. Let me know what I can do to help support you. Have you spoken to Francisco and Orlando yet?" asked Laura.

"Not yet, I've been formulating it and need a few more details before I approach them. But they are hard workers and I'm confident the promise of regular income will convince them to participate."

"Before we head back to Heredia, is it possible to make one last stop at the cemetery? I'd like to say a last goodbye to Gabriel."

"That sounds like a good idea. I'd love a bit of time there myself since I was sick after his funeral," Daniela said.

At the cemetery, they walked up to his gravesite. Laura talked to him and thanked him for everything he had showed her and for watching over her and Daniela until the arrests could be made. She placed a white lily on top of the burial box and walked away.

***

The day had come for her to fly back home. Antonio took her to the airport so they could say their final goodbyes. "I've really enjoyed our time together and hate to see it end. Do you think you'll be able to come visit me in California soon? I can't wait to show you my home," Laura said.

"I can get some time off in a couple of months. I think September. Would that be a good time?"

"I'll make it work, just give me a date. You have my home number and my email. I know long distance relationships can be tough, and I know your job will keep you busy. But I'm willing to try if you are."

"I promise I'll call you as often as I can."

"Let the prosecutor know I'm willing to testify at trial. I'll see if I can get in touch with Bianca and Anna and encourage them to testify too. They haven't responded to my emails though."

"Have you decided what you're going to do about your job?" Antonio asked.

"I made a promise to complete a certain amount of time in exchange for the benefit of giving me the sabbatical. I'll honor that. I did decide to volunteer with *Turtle Island Restoration Project* a couple of weekends a month. I hope that will lead me into some advocacy work. I liked working with Daniela on the proposals and the phone calls needed for the MINAE meetings. I'm hoping that translates into a new career."

"What about your ex-husband?"

"What about him? I'm done with him. I have no reason to communicate with him. He's probably too busy gambling and drinking to know that I've left the country. This experience has taught me the importance of keeping family and friends close. I consider everyone here to be family, and I'll be putting more effort into my family at home. Did you know I have a sister? We don't talk often, but I'll start by mending that relationship. My husband was part of the reason we became estranged."

They held hands and nuzzled often until the time came for her to go through security. "I hate saying goodbye. I'm thankful the universe conspired to bring us together."

"Call me when you get home, I don't care what time it is. I want to know you're home safe."

"Okay."

Tears formed as she turned to walk to her gate. It would be a long, long flight home.

The True Story

On May 30, 2013, Jairo Mora Sandoval, 26, was murdered on Playa Moin north of Puerto Limón. He was on the night patrol with four eco-volunteers looking for leatherback sea turtles. Three of the volunteers were from the United States and one was from Spain. It had been reported that the volunteers were kidnapped, sexually assaulted and dropped off at a deserted shack. Their belongings had been confiscated. However, it had been reported that two men stayed behind to watch the women, then released them.

Jairo was beaten, stripped and dragged behind his vehicle on Playa Moin. He died of asphyxiation from sand found in his system. Jairo was a conservationist who worked for *WIDECAST*, now Latin American Sea Turtles (LAST). He and a friend had previously been threatened with AK-47s and warned to stop the beach patrols. Jairo did post to his Facebook page and met with a reporter from *La Nación* in hopes of increasing support and security on the beach.

Turtle Island Restoration Project-Seaturtle.org, did offer a $10,000 reward for information and conviction of persons involved in this kidnapping and murder. A conservationist from this organization had been in Costa Rica to work with volunteers the day prior to the murder. This individual created the petition posted on line and they did garner the 137,000 signatures from 150 nations that was delivered to the Costa Rican Consulate in California.

Rainforest Radio is a real radio station that has a sister broadcasting network out of Los Angeles California. They are located on the Osa Peninsula and are involved with conservation stories as well as other news related to areas throughout Costa Rica.

The ad campaign for educating Ticos on turtle eggs not being aphrodisiacs is also real and was developed shortly after the murder of Jairo.

The Judicial Police arrested seven men for the kidnappings and murder two months after Jairo's death. One of the suspects had entered into the Witness Protection Program. They served one-year detention before coming to trial. On May 31, 2015 (two years after the death) the verdict was not guilty based on incomplete evidence, mishandling of evidence, and an ineffective investigation that provided reasonable doubt as its reason for their acquittal. This verdict brought global outrage and the prosecutors requested a new trial. An appeals court ordered a new trial in January 2016. Four of the seven men were found guilty and will serve 50 years, maximum allowed by Costa Rican law.

Turtle egg poaching continues on several beaches throughout Costa Rica (especially on the Caribbean side), and throughout the world. More and better armed security have been increased on Playa Moin and in national parks. Attacks on conservationists and volunteers do still occur throughout Costa Rica and the world.

To learn more about sea turtles and how to help, or to make a donation you can go to *Turtle Island Restoration Network or Seaturtles.org.*

Acknowledgements:

This multi-year project had more components and lessons than I ever expected or imagined, but has been a rewarding challenge. I would not have been able to accomplish this without the following:

Jerry Felts and Suzanne Jackson, thank you for introducing me to Costa Rica. That trip re-opened my channel of creativity and helped me to refocus on the simple pleasures of life and spending time on those things that enrich me.

To my husband Fred, thank you for your unwavering support. You've listened to my ideas, doubts, excitements. You've lived through me talking about my characters as if we lived with them. You've proof-read, made suggestions, assisted with research.

Sanctuary Cruises, Moss Landing, CA, specifically for the fund-raising tour supporting Christopher Pincetich, Ph.D., Turtle Island Restoration Network to raise awareness and funds for the critically endangered Pacific Leatherback Sea Turtle. Christopher new Jairo, and I gained valuable knowledge from chatting with him.

Tico Times- English news and reports re: Jairo Mora Sandoval, the drug arrests in the country, and other culturally related stories that have inspired and directed me in my research.

Other sources of news and research:
Costa Rican Times, Daily Star, La Nación, Rainforest Radio
AngloInfo, Costa Rica
TheRealCostaRica.com, Fodor's Costa Rica 2010 edition
SWOT (State of the Worlds Sea Turtles)
Seaturtles.org
Capitol Crimes.Org and Cindy Sample, especially, for her knowledge, encouragement and technical information regarding the steps to becoming a published writer. Truly a chance meeting of Karma. Michele Drier your mentorship and direction have been indispensable to me and I'm so grateful for your assistance.

To my beta readers: Dennis Carly, Linda Gustin, Fritzi Knese, Lori Ann Pearson, you read an early version of this story and your feedback was instrumental in helping me find the better path. Dana Ugrinich, your feedback aided in the final polish.

To my critique group: Richard Meredith, Karen Phillips, Nuvia Sandoval, and Emma Schwartz, your input and suggestions were much appreciated and I've learned so much from working with each of you.

Author Bio

 L.D. Markham is a trainer for the California Department of Justice (DOJ), Attorney General's Office. She also teaches business writing and proofreading classes and contributes to the DOJ quarterly newsletter *Justice Journal*. She has written training curriculum, narrative project memos, resumes, and short stories.
A life changing trip to Costa Rica inspired her debut novel.
Ms. Markham is a member of the national Sister's in Crime mystery writer's organization, Sacramento's Capitol Crimes writing group, and GUPPIES (also a part of Sister's in Crime). She enjoys travel, playing the piano, and currently resides in Sacramento, CA.
Follow LDMarkham online:
Twitter: @ldmarkhamwrites
Facebook:https://www.facebook.com/ldmarkhambooks/
website: ldmarkhambooks.com

Made in the USA
San Bernardino, CA
20 November 2018